The Green City

by Emily Thomas

First published in Great Britain in 2008
by Griffin Publishing Associates

Copyright © 2008 Emily Thomas

Names, characters and related indicia are copyright and trademark
Copyright © 2008 Emily Thomas

Emily Thomas has asserted his moral rights
to be identified as the author

A CIP Catalogue of this book is available from
the British Library

ISBN 978-0-9558955-0-0

All rights reserved; no part of this publication may be reproduced or
transmitted by any means, electronic, mechanical, photocopying or otherwise
without the written permission of the publisher.

Printed and bound in
Great Britain by Biddles Ltd,
King's Lynn, Norfolk

*For my friends and family,
who gave me the space to make this possible.*

'He undergirds and transcends, that He encompasses and penetrates all other things... Perhaps the supreme nature exists in place or time in a way that does not prevent him from existing as a whole all at once in individual places or times'.

St Anselm (Monologion & Proslogion).

PROLOGUE

The mind drifts in ether, tugged past sunken stars into ever darker swathes of sea-green. Everything here is green. The creature observes its world through a bottle-green lens, accustomed now to the way the shadows shade to indigo and the star-coronas are edged with silver.

This liquid, starry firmament has no limits but the mind is still at the mercy of tides: pushed at one moment up into white froth and at another sucked down into darkness. Despite the tides there is no sound here, the very absence of which generates a low ringing in the creature's ears. Just as sound is absent so is form – the few slivers of light that cast their pale shafts this deep fail to illuminate the creature. The mind is not something that can be illuminated.

The creature is happy to rest in the dark, happy to be tugged from one swathe of sea-green to another, until something so monstrous happens in the world of sunken lights below it is unwillingly called back, back and far away from its dimly lit seas…

CHAPTER 1

The body swung lazily from the rafters, the man's white hair gently brushing the tiles. Feet upright, ankles lashed to a wooden beam. Yellow morning sunlight illuminated the curling feet of the corpse: white skin creased like thin baking-paper, neatly trimmed nails and smudges of dirt on both soles. The rope was knotted around his bare ankles and dark leg hairs could be seen protruding from underneath the corduroy trousers. Dust motes danced around the legs in shafts of buttery sunlight and the shrine was quiet except for the droning of the bees outside.

Bunny sagged against the wall, her heart hammering in her chest. She swallowed convulsively twice and tasted vomit at the back of her throat. She turned her head away from the corpse until her breathing steadied. She did not want to look at the body of her father.

Bunny's day had *started* as it usually did. She'd woken up when the alarm sounded at
7:00am and lay in bed for a few moments luxuriating in the quiet of her little flat above the flower shop. She'd washed her sheets the day before and they felt all crisp and clean, still smelling lightly of lavender detergent. She stretched out naked in them before crawling into the shower. The hot water turned her blond hair dark and pasted it against her narrow frame. When she emerged from the bathroom to dress she selected a pair of woollen trousers in green that matched her eyes. On top she wore a plain black v-neck; as a primary schoolteacher she did not have to wear a suit. She tied up her shoulder-length hair in a bun and applied a little mascara. She was twenty-four and pretty, in a bookish sort of way. Once dressed Bunny wandered into the kitchen and cracked two eggs straight into a frying pan, giving them a quick whisk with a fork. Floorboards creaked as

she moved. She took two pieces of bread out of the freezer and put them in the toaster before switching on the kettle. While her breakfast cooked she darted into the lounge to make sure all her papers were ready for the day's lessons. The lounge was the cosiest room in the flat: it was full of bookcases, flowerpots and prints by Monet and Chagall. Her home was tidy except for the clothes draped over the sofa and the books scattered over the coffee table. She came back out of the lounge carrying her smart cardigan over her briefcase.

By the time she came back her breakfast was ready: using a knife she speared the popped-up toast and put it on a plate, flipped the eggs onto the toast and made her coffee. She ate her breakfast quickly and neatly, staring out of the window onto a higgledy-piggledy field of rooftops. Once she'd finished the food she drained the dregs of her coffee, put on the cardigan and tucked her briefcase under one arm. She picked up her car keys and walked from her front door down the outside steps to street level. The Yale clicked in time to her smart kitten heels.

The package sitting on the doorstep addressed to 'Miss Beatrice Eury' was the first unusual thing. It was slightly smaller than a shoebox, wrapped in brown paper and tied up with string. The three stamps were postmarked Shropshire and it was adorned with her father's looping handwriting. Bunny knelt down carefully to pick it up and turned it over slowly in her hands. Why was her father sending her a present? It was the middle of August – too late for her birthday and too soon for Christmas. Frowning slightly she walked back up the stairwell holding the parcel. She always allowed an extra five minutes for her drive to work – she had time to open this now.

When she re-entered her flat she put the parcel down carefully on the kitchen table and seated herself. Curiously she began ripping at the paper and when she finally uncovered the contents she sat stock still with her mouth open in an 'O' shape.

What *was* this?

The parcel contained whole reams of documents bound together by a rubber band: pink medical notes, internet print-outs, notebooks and journal articles. On top of them was a handwritten letter from her father. It began: 'My darling daughter, I have done a terrible thing.' Paper-clipped to the back of the letter was a passport. It had the usual red cover embossed with gold, but it was a fake. On the back page, underneath a photograph of Bunny, was the name 'Laura Elizabeth Rourke'. Bunny closed the passport with a snap and swallowed; she had no idea how her father had obtained it.

She set the letter safely under the sugar bowl and began pulling the other documents out of their elastic band. There were lots of papers on philosophy and psychology, some had been ripped out of journals and others had been printed off the website *j-stor*. Many were highlighted and annotated in her father's handwriting. One of the papers was by her father – "A Metaphysician's Take on Telekinesis" – and it seemed to be offering a philosophical explanation for spoon-bending. Another sheaf of papers turned out to be a set of engineering diagrams for some sort of brain scanning machine; there were several drafts of these and although Bunny understood little of the detail it was easy to see that the design had been re-worked many times. There were also two sets of medical notes, one of which had a Polaroid stapled to it. Bunny studied the patient's face carefully but had no idea who he was. She tried to make sense of what she was reading but she was neither a scientist nor a philosopher and she found most of the text impenetrable. She turned back to her father's letter and tried to decide what to do. In it he told her – in no uncertain terms – to leave the country. Not to try to find him in his home in Pottersby.

Bunny re-read those last words and set her jaw. She picked up her car keys and strode to the front door, her briefcase with its precious lesson plans forgotten underneath the table. She was going to help her father.

She drove her Mini like a mad woman, dashing round corners and honking her horn. The drive out of Lowestoft seemed to take interminably long; Bunny bit her lip and pounded her fists on the steering wheel at every set of traffic lights. It was rush-hour and the roads were chock-full of mothers driving their children to school in Land Rovers and businessmen on their way to work. After twenty minutes the traffic eased and the buildings on either side of the road began to thin. Gradually the seaside town petered out completely and Bunny headed firmly inland, the wide road surrounded by bright green fields and low hills. She cruised along at 80mph, her eyes flickering down to the speedometer every time she pressed her foot a little harder on the accelerator. To get to her father's home in Pottersby she literally had to drive across the breadth of England, taking the A14 towards Birmingham and then the A5 towards the English-Welsh border. It was a solid four hour drive but Bunny beat down the miles remorselessly. The hot summer sun bleached the tarmac ahead of her and created a shimmering on the horizon.

Once she passed the outskirts of Wolverhampton and Shrewsbury the roads got narrower and were surrounded by butter-yellow cornfields and herds of frothy white sheep. At this point she had to start obeying the speed limit for fear of skidding off into ditches. As she drove her thoughts turned irrevocably towards her father.

Robert Eury was a tall, lean man with a serious face and a quick smile. His wife had died when Bunny was little and the loss had nearly destroyed him; he'd left his Chair in Oxford and taken himself and his infant daughter deep into the countryside to Pottersby. There he found a refuge from the world, a cottage so deep in the woods one couldn't even drive the last half mile to it. The peace of the green trees had soothed him. Bunny had grown up there – it was where she had acquired her nickname – and she had been home-schooled by her father until the age of eleven. She remembered those early years with joy and fleeting impressions: of sitting cross-legged in her father's study as he taught her to read, playing amongst leafy green shadows and mossy oaks, reading Enid Blyton in her beautiful attic bedroom and seeing the stars out of the large windows.

When she had turned eleven Bunny was sent to boarding school and the lazy timbre of her days changed. She made friends for the first time, discovered whole new worlds of television and girly magazines. She thrived in her new environment, attaining excellent grades and going on to study English Literature at university. It was when she got to Warwick that Bunny first began to understand the man her father was when he wasn't being her father. She'd supposed that in an abstract way she'd always known he was a philosopher – he spent lots of time writing books in his study – but it wasn't until she became a student that she understood what that meant.

One day in the university library, on a whim, Bunny typed her father's name into Google. It was past 11:00pm – the dark and empty library was like a closed museum – so there was no one around to see her mouth drop open when the search engine returned 1,033 hits. With growing amazement Bunny repeated her search in the library catalogue and discovered that over the last forty years her father had published eleven books and forty-eight papers. Two thirds of them had been written before she was born.

The next day Bunny 'accidentally' took a wrong turn in the Social Sciences building and ended up in the Philosophy Department. While asking a post-grad for directions she found herself mentioning her father.

"Have you ever heard of a philosopher called Robert Eury?"

"Eury? Yeah, of course! I think he's dead now, though."

"Really?" Bunny couldn't help but smile. *"I read a book of his fairly recently. I'm pretty certain he's still alive."*

"Ah well, you might be right. It's just that all the good ones are generally dead."

Bunny laughed and before she knew it she was being dragged down to an office at the end of the corridor. There she was told she simply had to meet Dr James Mackie, because he was 'just the world's greatest living expert' on Eury and all his works. No introductions seemed to be necessary once the post-grad explained which philosopher Bunny was interested in.

"Ah, Eury!" *The professor had exclaimed.* "What is it you want to know?" *Mackie was a surprisingly young man with a shock of dark hair and a twinkle in his eye that reminded Bunny of her father.*

Before Bunny could reply, the post-grad answered for her. "We want to know if he's dead or not."

Mackie laughed. "No, Eury's not dead. He's probably one of the greatest living metaphysicians the world has."

"Do you know him?" *Bunny asked.*

"Not well, but I met him once at a conference in Oxford. Brilliantly clever. One of those people that you can see their brain firing off – you know, all the cogs whirring behind their eyes – when they talk. Horrifically bright. Mad as a hatter, of course, but then all the best philosophers are."

"You like his work?"

"Very much." *Mackie grinned.* "Probably because it's all so barking. But good barking, if you see what I mean!" *He lit a cigarette.* "The wonderful thing about his work – and believe me, I've spent a lot of time trying to do this in various papers – is that although it's all so crazy it's hard to just put your finger on why, *say there, that's where it all goes silly*. And of course his theories are all so beautifully constructed, so elegant, you almost don't want to."

"What's so silly about them"? *Bunny asked, unable to imagine her sensible, thoughtful father writing anything that wasn't.*

"Well, for starters he's a modal realist." *The professor took a deep drag on his cigarette.* "You know what that means?"

"No?"

"Well, it means he thinks that everything that is possible exists. Literally. Not in some abstract, hypothetical way that allows us to talk about modality without actually having to worry about it but in a real, solid, physical way. Other possible worlds, just sitting there on some faraway plane. Very Star Trek."

"I had no idea."

"Oh yes. And that's just his view on modality! Some of his theories of consciousness get even weirder. Did you know, for example, that he once submitted a paper to Philosophical Quarterly explaining how, if a group of schizophrenics all independently identified an invisible creature sitting in the same part of a room, and there was no other explanation, then that must mean that there really was something sitting in the room? Something that only the schizophrenics could see? It was rejected, of course, no philosophy journal would publish something like that, although I think it may actually have gone out in a psychology one."

"Wow."

"And then there's his supervenience theory to explain why the mind and brain are identical... I mean, well, that's all okay I suppose, but the idea that consciousness could emerge from Lego? Come on."

"Lego?" Bunny was utterly confused.

"You know, it joins in with his argument for necessary physicalism." Mackie caught Bunny's blank expression. "Look, Eury's a physicalist, yes? That means he thinks that everything in this world is explainable by science. Or some future science. The point is, there's nothing that won't one day be explained by science. All physicalists think that. But what most physicalists don't say is that physicalism is necessarily true – they think our world might have contained stuff not explainable by science but it just happens not to."

"Non-physical stuff like souls," the post-grad interjected.

"Exactly. But Eury argues not just that our world doesn't contain any of that weird stuff, but that it couldn't. He thinks that physicalism is necessarily true. It's an extremely unusual position."

"You're not explaining the Lego," said the post-grad with a grin.

"All right, all right. Going back to the Lego." Mackie grinned too. "This is where it gets extra weird. Eury's Lego Theory is a formulation of emergent consciousness. He thinks that the mind is identical to the brain and that consciousness can emerge in any physical configuration that reaches a suitable level of complexity. Even in Lego."

"But that's mad!"

Mackie chuckled and stubbed out his cigarette. "I know. But isn't it great?"

And so the conversation had gone on. Bunny had enjoyed finding out what a celebrity her father was and the fact that people thought he was just a little bit crazy made her smile. When she'd returned home at the end of that term she'd found herself treating her father with something approaching awe and she'd coaxed him into talking about his current work. Robert had been surprised and gratified that his only child, who'd shown no previous interest in philosophy, was coming around to the idea.

After her degree she qualified as a primary school teacher and eventually managed to get a place to study for her Newly Qualified Teacher's year in Lowestoft. She missed her father dearly but the school was excellent and she liked the idea of living in a seaside town. She'd stayed there even after she'd completed her training and although she had always intended to move closer to her father she simply hadn't got around to it yet.

Once Bunny crossed Offa's Dyke and began getting really close to Pottersby her progress slowed to a crawl; sometimes it seemed to her that her father's home was remote not just in miles but in time. Over the last twenty mile stretch the roads were little more than dirt tracks and there were no signposts or telephone boxes. The last group of houses that numbered more than a dozen had been passed fifteen minutes before. She was forced to drive at around 15mph, high hedges scratching at her windows and the sound of bees penetrating over the engine noise. After an eternity of this the hedgerows suddenly fell away and a group of houses were revealed nestled deep on the bottom of a wooded valley.

Pottersby was well below sea level and encroached upon by trees on all sides, three of which were constituted by steep hills. The fourth side extended north-west, into the depths of Bayleir Forest. The only road to Pottersby approached from the south and Bunny now carefully followed that winding, muddy track down to the cluster of houses at the bottom of the valley. Pottersby had a grand total of eighty-four residents, one shop/post office and one red public telephone. All the residents were over fifty and nearly all of them lived in the rambling old cottages lining the track at the centre of the hamlet. Half a dozen, including her father, lived even more remotely either higher up in the heavily wooded hills of the valley or deeper in the forest. Post could be collected only from the little office and anyone in search of a gas station or bank would have at least a twenty minute drive ahead of them. Despite its remoteness you could understand why people would choose to live here – the place was beautiful. As Bunny drove through the small group of houses she saw curtains twitching and the odd head bobbing out from the gardens but she didn't have time to stop and exchange pleasantries. When she reached the end of the line of houses she took a left-hand turn onto a track that was barely sketched into the woods.

Bayleir Forest was also beautiful; the sun gleamed off the dark hues of the trees and white blossoms winked from leafy shadows. Trees overhung the rough track, their mossy branches criss-crossing to form a forest-tunnel. Leaves and bluebells brushed the car's wing-mirrors. Bunny cut her speed to 5mph, mindful of the uneven stones that scattered the ground and the stream that ran intermittently along her right side. Birds twittered overhead and the blue wing of a dragonfly glinted as it caught a shaft of sunlight. The trees were all different shades of green.

After ten minutes of driving she reached a round clearing in the middle of the forest – this was as far as she could go by car. The last part of the journey to her father's cottage always had to be completed on foot. She parked her car carefully and got out, wincing when her clean heels sank into the soft earth. She left her parcel and her cardigan on the passenger seat and slid out of the car. She didn't bother to lock it. She began walking north-east out of the clearing, taking care to follow the overgrown foot path so as to do least damage to her smart woollen trousers. She'd been walking for only a few minutes before she came to the forest shrine.

The low stone building loomed out of the trees, a testament to a different era. Once upon a time it had probably been pagan but at some point over the past centuries it had acquired a Christian veneer. As Bunny walked closer to its white-washed walls she peered in through the rough, open doorway. The shrine was tiny – it contained a single alcove in which rested a statue of the Virgin Mary. The floor was made of uneven paving slabs and the plaster on the walls was cracking and falling away. It was beautifully illuminated: the single window was slanted, set into the join between wall and ceiling at the perfect angle to catch the bright midday sun.

Bunny didn't see the statue or the window. She saw only her father's body, swinging gently from a wooden beam.

She tried desperately not to be sick. The idea of vomiting in this place – of befouling it further – was repulsive.

When she felt more in control she forced herself to step forward and knelt down to peer into the corpse's face. The body was undeniably her father's, despite the fact his facial muscles were distorted by lying so slack and upside down. His features were all contorted: the mouth half-open to show his teeth and his corn-blue eyes staring into nothing. His skin was dark purple, the colour of squashed grapes. Blood covered the chest of his worn blue shirt and the room contained an unpleasant over-ripe odour.

Bunny padded softly backwards, her eyes wide and her thin shoulders shaking. Her jaw worked as she continued to hold back vomit. She swayed slightly and held her car keys so tight they began to gouge into her palm. A noise came from somewhere behind her but her eyes didn't even flicker. She continued to swallow and couldn't seem to stop trembling. The noise came again – louder this time – a strange scraping sound. Bunny didn't react until it sounded a third time and when she did finally turn around she let out a guttural moan, clutching the keys even tighter.

In its little alcove the statue of the Virgin Mary was wobbling from side-to-side like an unsteady bowling pin, its base swivelling clockwise on the chalky stone as if it were glued there and someone was trying to ease it free. Suddenly it rotated one last time until it began to float, very slowly and completely soundlessly, towards Bunny. The statue's painted eyes and benevolent smile took on a sinister aura and Bunny shrieked, making a stumbling run towards the doorway. Hanging there, blocking her exit, was a formless black shape. The black thing hung there like a cartoon ghost, a dark cloud that roughly defined a head and a body. It hung five or six inches above the ground. Bunny stood rooted to the spot, caught between the wraith and the statue, her eyes wide and her mouth open as if about to scream. Her pupils were wide as she turned to look at one threat and then back towards the other. The temperature in the shrine plummeted and steam began rising off the walls. A thin layer of frost rimmed the empty alcove and the blood on her father's chest began to freeze.

The wraith moved towards her and Bunny backed against the wall, the statue forgotten. The thing came closer and stretched out one of its black, spindly arms. Where it brushed the plaster the white layers cracked and dissolved into dust. Bunny stood paralysed as the shadowy appendage came closer, the wraith only inches from her face, and then it moved to touch her shoulder. Pain shot through her left arm – the sleeve of her top had been scorched straight through – and the skin felt frozen and burning all at once. Bunny shrieked and tried to slide away but the wraith slid with her… and then behind them both the statue moved again.

With a noise like a *fizz* the statue shot straight towards them and hit the wraith square in its middle. The statue disintegrated into flying black shards but the wraith moved back away from Bunny and she ran for it. She sprinted through the undergrowth back to her car, scratching her legs on brambles and clutching her keys to her chest. She tripped over a gorse bush and knew without looking back that the black thing was following her; she picked herself up with a cry and stumbled onwards. Her trousers snagged on thorns and her hair caught on branches but she barely felt them – the only thing she did feel was the burning in her arm. When she got back to the clearing she fumbled with her car door and saw the wraith gliding through the trees behind her; with a sob she slid into the driver's seat and jammed the keys into the ignition. Mercifully the Mini started first time and she revved the engine hard, shooting out of the clearing with a squeal of tires. Bunny pushed her foot down on the accelerator and raced along the forest track - she didn't slow even when she saw the wraith falling behind through the trees in her rear-view mirror.

Even as she drove something followed her.

CHAPTER 2

The mind performs a whiplash turn in the darkness, sensing movement in a place where no movement should be. With great effort – because the place is very far away – it begins the difficult journey down through the green and pulls itself towards a distant set of underwater lights…

* * *

Blaine was jerked awake with a *thwap* to the side of his head. His left ear rang in pain and he swore aloud as he fuzzily dragged himself out of sleep. The pain came again – a harder blow this time – and he blearily opened his eyes to see that he was being attacked by a red-faced man with a traffic cone.

"Hey!" Blaine put his hands out but the man continued to raise the cone over his shoulder for another hit.

Blaine's body was half-tangled in bed sheets and beside him a woman was screaming. Understanding dawned as the veils of alcohol parted. He began to climb out of bed, fending off blows from the traffic cone. His attacker was dressed in some sort of traffic uniform and was crying something about unfaithfulness.

"You never told me you were married," he growled to the aging blond beside him.

As he turned his head to talk the cone caught him painfully on the jaw and Blaine swung angrily around to punch the man.

"I'm leaving!" Blaine shouted, but the man had already slipped into unconsciousness. Without a backwards look Blaine pulled on his jeans and left.

He walked back through the streets of London in the eerie pre-dawn light, the grimy buildings of the East End softened by the blue twilight. The world was quiet and empty; over the hour long walk he passed only two other people. It seemed that even the homeless crept out of sight at this hour. The tall streetlamps made the pavements glow and his footsteps echoed on the old slabs. He got a glimpse of his tall, dark reflection in a shop doorway and scrubbed at his chin. He needed a shave.

Blaine could have returned to his flat but his office was closer, so in the end he walked there. As he approached the drab building the first rays of sunlight climbed over the horizon and made the dark windows wink like sinister eyes. He hated his office. The small part of the building Blaine rented was on the fourteenth floor and the lift, as usual, was broken. He climbed the stairs slowly and approached the door that announced the space beyond to be the home of 'O'Dwyer Investigations'. The square window of frosted glass set into the door was dirty and Blaine stared at it as he put his key in the lock. When the door swung open he collapsed into the armchair behind his desk. The office felt even smaller than it was. It contained a bookshelf, two armchairs and a desk. Another small door set into the corner led to a tiled bathroom. It smelt faintly of cigarette smoke and everything was covered in dust. The blinds were already drawn and even if they weren't the heavy dust on the windowpanes would prevent the morning sun from creeping in. Blaine cleared a space on the desk: pushing away paper files, tabbed books and dirty coffee mugs. Once he'd revealed a patch of the scratched wood underneath he put his head on his arms and slept.

He was rudely awoken four hours later by a crash in the hallway outside. Blaine had been dreaming of Lilly again. He grunted and tried to shake the nightmare off as he blearily peered at his *faux* train station clock. It clicked and stuttered as its tumblers revolved to show that the time was 10:02am. He unfolded his stiff frame from the armchair and opened the door onto the corridor, where he collected the sheaf of letters that had been jammed into the metal basket on the nearby wall. Blaine decided that he'd go through the post and then go over the road to Starbucks for a coffee and food. He re-entered the office and slammed the door closed with his foot. He sank back into his armchair and began flipping through the pile of envelopes. Most of the post was mundane: a telephone bill, an invoice for the replacement of his car window, half a dozen pieces of junk mail and a letter asking for his assistance in catching a thieving sales advisor.

It was the last letter that proved the most interesting. The envelope was heavy and creamy, the name and address handwritten. There was no stamp – it had been hand delivered. Blaine tilted his head to one side as he opened it. As he slit the envelope with his thin pocket knife a pink Compliments slip fell out. Blaine picked up the small piece of paper and studied it. In the top right hand corner was the logo and address of Faber Enterprises. In blue fountain pen were written the words: 'I will see you at midday, F'. Blaine actually turned the slip over, searching for more. When none was forthcoming he sat back in his chair and chewed a pen.

Two hours later Blaine stood on the steps of Faber Enterprises, an empty polystyrene cup in one hand and the remains of a bagel in the other. He finished the food while looking up at the buildings around him. Canary Wharf was a wealthy area where restored Victorian buildings and cutting-edge architecture nestled uncomfortably side by side. The skyscraper that housed Faber Enterprises was of the latter kind: the gigantic building was composed of steel and tinted blue glass, it looked like a jagged crystal rising proudly into the sky. The watery October sunlight glinted off the windows and behind the fogged glass he could see the silhouettes of office workers scurrying like ants. He imagined that Faber's offices would be high up in the penthouse suite. Before Blaine had left the East End he'd searched for Faber Enterprises on the internet. He'd discovered that the company was run by a single man: one Dr Gideon Faber. The scientist had recently undergone a meteoric rise to fame and money through success on the stock markets but before that he'd been a psychiatrist known only for his moderately successful self-help books. He had invested in many different companies including – most controversially – one that was trying to develop a fully artificial womb.

Blaine threw the litter from his breakfast into a nearby bin and entered the double revolving doors of the skyscraper. Within lay a lobby tiled in pink marble that reflected the elaborate chandeliers above. A sleek reception desk stood in the centre.

"Good afternoon sir, how can I help you?" The receptionist's soft Scottish accent was as sugary as her manicured nails.

"I have an appointment with Dr Faber."

The woman nodded and murmured something into her earpiece. A pale, thickset man appeared beside the desk.

"This is Eluf, one of Dr Faber's aides. He'll take you upstairs. If you could just sign the register?"

Blaine signed the proffered visitor's book and silently followed his guide into the lift. As the elevator doors closed he caught their reflection in the polished metal: Blaine was a tall man at five foot eleven but Eluf still towered over him. The aide had stiff blond hair, blue eyes and a very light tan. Blaine wondered what sort of point Faber was trying to make by greeting him with his bodyguard. Eluf punched some numbers into the lift's control panel and it began to rise smoothly upwards. Blaine stood straight and stared fixedly into space, stoically enduring the always unacknowledged intimacy of the elevator shaft. The mechanism chimed their arrival and a digital screen set into the wall above the doors showed that they had arrived on the top floor of the building.

"This way." Eluf stepped out of the lift without a backward glance and Blaine followed him.

Faber's offices were indeed on the top floor of the skyscraper. Blaine stepped out into a massive corridor with doors leading off in all directions and a long, thin window revealing clouds at the far end. Two security guards were stationed either side of the most central door and Eluf walked towards them. Soft words were spoken between the three of them and then the aide motioned Blaine towards the door.

"The doctor will see you now. Please step inside," Eluf said curtly.

Blaine nodded and when he approached the door it opened automatically. He stepped through and it snapped closed behind him with a *whoosh* of air on the back of his neck.

The chamber inside was beautiful. Faber's office was set into the top north-east corner of the skyscraper so that two of the walls and part of the ceiling were composed of blue tinted glass. This provided a god's eye view of the city and the cloudy sky. It would be especially striking at night, with the stars above and the city picked out in pinpricks of light below. The office was decorated with plush blue carpets and creamy wallpaper. It contained little furniture – just two dark bookshelves and a thick slab of oak that served as a desk. Blaine smelt the money hanging in the air and wondered, not for the first time, what he was doing here.

Gideon narrowed his eyes as he studied the man he'd brought before him. To date he'd hired five security firms – some legitimate, some not – to do the job he needed doing and so far all of them had failed. He'd decided to try another tack and had asked his advisors to prepare a list of the Private Investigators in the city that might be tempted to commit one very special crime for money. O'Dwyer Investigations had been near the top of that list. The PI did not just need the money, he had a history of vigilante activity. Despite the risk of exposure Gideon had decided to hire him.

Blaine O'Dwyer was a tall man with broad shoulders and a flat stomach.

Gideon knew from the file in front of him that he was thirty-eight. He had a ruggedly handsome face with a wide forehead, straight nose and square jaw. Black hair curled softly around his ears and that coupled with his blue eyes betrayed his Irish heritage. He wore jeans with an open-necked white shirt; chest hair poked out of the top of the shirt and the sleeves were folded back to his elbows. There was a slight bulge by his right hip and he stood with the relaxed watchfulness Gideon associated with military men.

"Do you like the view?" Gideon stood up at the desk behind Blaine.

Blaine swung around from the windows and belatedly noted his host. Dr Faber was a tall, thin man with greying hair. He had a hawk nose and pale blue eyes that shone out of his leathery face.

"Very much." A wisp of an Irish accent came through in his voice.

Gideon held the eye-contact for a moment before moving towards his drinks cabinet. "Brandy?"

"No, thank you. Not while I'm on business."

"How quaint." Gideon poured himself a glass of the amber liquid and the ice cubes clinked as he returned to his desk to sit down.

Blaine became uncomfortably aware that there was only one chair in the room. "Quaint?"

"That you don't drink 'on business', even when you haven't the faintest idea what the business is."

Blaine realised that the desk and the small area around it was slightly raised, as if the doctor sat on a plinth. He felt that even though he was the only man standing he was the one being looked down upon.

"Dr Faber. What is it exactly you'd like me to do for you?"

Gideon swirled the brandy in his glass. "It depends. Are you as good an investigator as people say you are?"

"Sir -"

"I'm an old man. Indulge me."

Blaine cocked his head to one side. He'd spent thirteen years in the army, four in the police and three as a private investigator. "I'm probably better."

Gideon chuckled softly. "Okay then. I have a 'case' for you. A missing persons case. If you close it successfully for me I'll pay you half a million."

"What?" The figure cracked Blaine's composure. Half a million was a huge amount – it would pay for his flat twice over, allow him to leave his dingy office... "I generally charge by the hour."

"I know. But in return for the cash there is a catch."

Blaine swallowed and tried not to show how desperate he was for the money. "Which is?"

"Once you've found the missing person, I want you to make sure they stay missing."

Blaine blinked. "I'm an investigator, not a gun for hire."

"Perhaps not an assassin, no. But a vigilante?"

Blaine stayed silent this time, his jaw locked. He was remembering Lilly: her bloodied body on the green linoleum, the red nails and the lax nipples. He remembered the twist to her smile and the sucking noise the knife had made.

"I am only asking you to kill a killer," Faber continued into the silence.

"Who is he?" Blaine said slowly.

Gideon slid a single sheet of paper across the desk. It was a black and white photocopy of a passport.

"*She*," Gideon emphasised the pronoun, "is a murderess. She has been missing for nearly three months. Her name is Beatrice Eury."

After the meeting Blaine took the underground back across London and then walked the short distance to his flat. The cramped space was messy and needed a good clean. Blaine ignored the mess and had a quick shower. He took two aspirin for his headache and discovered a purple bump rising nicely behind his right ear – a temporary reminder of last night's conquest. Once he'd showered and re-dressed he sat down at his kitchen table to begin work on his latest case. He realised that before he could do so he had to clear the file already sitting on it: he'd followed the husband of a suspicious wife and had discovered the woman he was having an affair with. The file contained photographs as well as case notes. He should have called the wife first thing this morning so instead he did so now and received the expected torrent of abuse. It didn't matter – he always asked in these cases for his fee to be paid in advance.

That done he cleared the table and studied the photocopy Faber had given him. The passport was open at the page with the owner's photograph and details on, so Blaine had the missing woman's name and address to go on. In black pen someone had scribbled the word 'Bunny' next to her name. Blaine thought that the nickname suited the woman better. The passport photograph showed a young woman smiling into the camera: her pale blond hair bounced in loose ringlets around her face and matched the merriment that danced in her green eyes. Pale skin, slightly flushed cheeks and a delicate bone structure completed the look of a young English Rose. Blaine surmised that the photograph was a little old – the file also said that Bunny was twenty-four. Her listed address was in Lowestoft in East Anglia and he got out a UK road map before packing a small bag.

Before Blaine left he called one of his old friends from the force. Peirce often slipped Blaine police files for a small fee.

The phone rang twice before being picked up. "Inspector Blackwell."

"Hey, Peirce? It's me. I've got some work for you."

There was a pause; perhaps Peirce was smoking. "Shoot."

"I need the info from a missing persons file, name of Beatrice Eury. Whatever's in it – police record, credit cards receipts, anything."

"You've been hired on it?"

"Yeah."

"I should have it for you by tomorrow."

"Cool. Thanks buddy."

"I'll call ya."

"I know. Speak soon." Smiling, Blaine clicked his phone shut and checked his watch. It had just gone 2:30pm – there ample time to get to Lowestoft so that he could search Bunny's house. He wasn't sure what he hoped to find there but he felt that if he were to find any clues as to where she might have run to her home would be a good place to start.

Blaine enjoyed the drive out of the city and north up the coast, music blaring from the speakers of his MGF Rover and the soft-top down so that the wind could ruffle his hair. The afternoon got sunnier as it wore on and the A12 was blissfully free of traffic. He drove fast and carelessly, singing along to the *Wasp* song on the radio. He tried not to think about the fact he was driving to kill a woman he'd never met – the second woman he'd ever killed. He tried not to wonder if he'd have done it for nothing, tried not to think about Lilly. Whenever his thoughts turned towards her he jacked the volume of the radio up higher and concentrated on the three hour drive.

When he finally arrived on the outskirts of Lowestoft he parked outside the nearest accommodation he could find. A sign just before the car park of the Swan Hotel announced that he was 'Welcome to Lowestoft – the most Easterly Town in Britain'. Blaine swung his bag out of the boot and entered the reception area of the building. There he paid £60 for a double room with ensuite and dropped his bag off. On the way out of the hotel he asked the tired receptionist for directions to Eccles Street. That done, he got back into his car and headed towards the town centre.

Blaine had some trouble finding the right street and twice drove past the Esplanade that fronted on the sea before discovering the narrow road. He was forced to park some distance away and then jogged back over the cobbles. When he arrived back on the street he had more trouble finding the actual house. 28 Eccles Street was not a residential building but a flower shop. Confused, he checked the address again and realised it must refer to a flat *above* the flower shop. The shop itself was beautifully decorated, with the frontage in mock Tudor style and full of hanging baskets that surrounded lead-paned windows and an open wooden door. On the window sill sat a row of pumpkins: each had a carved ghoulish face and a candle inside. After another moment of confusion Blaine realised that it was Halloween tonight.

Beside the shop entrance was a much smaller, narrower door that was locked. Blaine looked around furtively and reminded himself that it was nearly three months since Bunny had disappeared - even if the police had been watching her home they wouldn't be any more. He ducked into the well of shadow created by the inset door and slipped his lock picking kit out of his pocket. Working mainly by touch he slid the pick into the keyhole. It was fairly simple and clicked open after a few seconds. Blaine pushed the door open and eased his way inside. He was faced with a dark staircase that stank of flowers. He supposed it was the sort of thing that might appeal to a woman. At the top of the stairs he was faced with another door – the Yale was even easier to pick – and after he'd opened that he stepped up into Bunny's flat.

The kitchen was light and airy even though it was small. A wooden table dominated the room but the walls were painted a friendly yellow and the pale pine cabinets matched the floorboards. The room was full of pot plants – they were clustered on the deep window sill over the sink, on the table and all over the work surfaces. Blaine opened up a few of the cupboards at random: brightly coloured, mismatched crockery winked out of one and tins of soup and tomatoes poked out of another. The room was clean and tidy except for a cluster of dirty coffee mugs in the sink - Blaine would bet his eye-teeth they'd been left there by previous investigators.

He moved into the lounge where the plant theme continued. The walls in here were painted a darker shade of yellow and a brown leather corner-sofa dominated the room. The floorboards were partially covered with a red rug and the walls were decorated with prints and books. He recognised a few of the pictures – there were some by Monet – but very few of the books. There was some fiction, lots of classical plays and one shelf devoted to philosophy. Leaning closer, he saw that several of the philosophy books were written by Robert Eury. Was he a relation?

Two doors led out from the lounge, one to a neatly kept bathroom and the other to her bedroom. The bedroom was also painted yellow and the double bed was covered with a dark red eiderdown. Pot plants also adorned the window sill in here and a large wardrobe was revealed to be full of skirts, tops and shoes. The pine chest of drawers contained underwear and t-shirts. The low bedside cabinet held a half-empty cup of tea, a novel with a bookmark on page sixty-eight and two Durex condoms. There was no box so Blaine had no idea how old the contraception was or whether the lover was current.

Returning to the lounge he investigated the piles of paper spilling over the coffee table. Anything of real interest would probably already have been taken but the leftovers could still give him some clues to her character. Sorting through, Blaine found that they were mainly lesson plans and print-outs of activities for children. On her passport her occupation was listed as 'Teacher'.

That sparked a thought: where was her computer? He pulled out his mobile and composed a brief text message to a young man he'd met while on the force. KT was a hacker, a slippery little bugger who'd narrowly escaped arrest during a drugs bust. He hadn't been a dealer, just a user who in return for his coke had often run computer-related errands for his suppliers. He'd escaped arrest by wiping all traces of those errands just before the bust took place. Blaine had taken an odd liking to the boy – had perhaps respected his expertise in a field that Blaine knew little about – and kept in contact over the years. Blaine occasionally paid him for small jobs. As far as he knew KT still lived in a gloomy bed-sit in the outskirts of London, surrounded by computer screens and *Loaded* pin-ups. Blaine's text was short: 'Hey KT, I have a job for you. Can you trace laptops? B.'

That done he settled himself on the sofa and began shuffling through the lesson plans, seeing notes on the best way to teach numeracy and basic world geography, a brief sketch of the costumes worn by Tudors and Stuarts. In one of the margins, next to a picture of a woman in a lacy, ruffled dress was the note: 'Wouldn't Abi be happy in this!' It was that note, more than the neatly-kept flat with its books and pictures, that made Blaine wonder about its inhabitant. How could a woman who wrote notes in the margin for her students be a killer? His thoughts returned to Lilly and he dismissed his misgivings. The old cliché returned: *What's a nice girl like you doing in a place like this?* Blaine sighed and began rifling through the drawers of a dresser on the far side of the room. His reverie was interrupted by the ringing of his mobile.

"Hello?"

"It's KT."

"Eleven minutes! That was fast." The kid must sit by his computer all day long.

"Yeah well, you know me." KT sounded like he was chewing and smiling at the same time. "So, this laptop, you have a model or IP address?"

"Um, no?"

"Do you know anything about it?"

"Just the name of the person it belonged to. She's gone missing and I'm trying to find her."

KT sighed. "B-man I need more than that if you want me to trace it. How 'bout a receipt for it, where it was bought?"

"No – wait." Blaine had just opened a drawer filled with receipts. "Hang on." He sorted through receipts for a microwave, hair straighteners and a DVD player before finding the right one. He read out the details. "You think that'll be enough?"

"Maybe. I'll see what I can do. It might cost a hundred or so if it's a real pain to track down."

"That's fine. Thanks mate."

"Catch ya later, B-man." KT hung up.

Blaine searched through the rest of the drawer but didn't find anything else of interest. With a sigh – so far this trip hadn't been desperately productive – he stacked the papers back neatly on the table and went into the kitchen.

Where he was hit, for the second time that day, on the back of the head. Blaine yelled but a second blow sent him reeling to the floor. He heard smashing glass as he crashed into the washing machine and his legs tangled in the feet of the table. He tasted blood on his tongue and he twisted on the floor to face his assailant even as he slid his gun out of its holster. He blinked to clear the blood out of his eyes and saw that the room was empty.

"What the -" Blaine started and then he saw the object in the window.

Night had fallen outside and so the pumpkin shone eerily orange in the dark. The candle within was lit and buttery light poured from its triangular eyes and jagged mouth. For a moment it hung suspended - framed by the broken window - and then it shot unerringly across the kitchen towards Blaine.

Blaine screamed as it hit him hard in the face, cracking across the bridge of his nose and exploding against his forehead. He felt rather than saw another flying across the room and he raised his gun and shot – two hard *cracks* – the second pumpkin and then a third until he was shooting blindly into a maelstrom of breaking fruit and wax and pulp.

CHAPTER 3

The creature senses forbidden information flowing through the indigo highways of the internet. It swivels in its starry ocean and with great care tries to focus on the activities of the little lights below. They are so small and quick it is difficult but if last night's warning had not been enough it would need to do more to protect its charge. The mammoth creature propels itself slowly through the green.

* * *

The next morning Blaine was awoken early by the harsh ringing of his mobile phone. He fumbled for the catch and answered it.

"I've got it!" KT said triumphantly. "*I know where she is.*"

Blaine tried to focus on that even though his head felt like a lead balloon. Last night he'd left the flat in a total mess, the kitchen covered in remains of pumpkin. He'd *mostly* convinced himself that they had been thrown in through the window by trick-or-treaters and were not the manifestation of Halloween ghosts. He was trying to forget the way the pumpkins had hovered in the window, the way they'd aimed straight for him. Once the onslaught of pumpkins had ceased he'd slipped from the door quickly – he was afraid that someone might have heard the gunfire. He'd driven straight back to his hotel and collapsed.

"I'm a little tired right now KT, do you think it could wait a few hours?" Blaine blearily tried to focus on the alarm clock beside the bed – the display read 4:18am.

"Sorry, man." There was a pause. "I been doing some lines. You want me to call back?"

"No, actually I guess it's fine." Blaine swung his legs round off the bed and reached for the glass of water on the bedside cabinet. "I'm up now." He swallowed some water. "Hit me with it."

"You'll never guess where she is."

"Surprise me."

"Guess."

"I don't know, KT, it's bloody early. Glasgow, Salisbury, Liverpool. Where?"

"Japan."

"*What?*" Blaine slammed the glass down. "Are you serious?"

"Very."

"How the fuck did she get there? Wait. You're not telling that *she's* there – just that her laptop is?"

"Well, yeah. But she'll be where her laptop is, right? I traced the model through her credit card and after much technological wrangling got her IP. And get this – she used it the very night before she disappeared on an origami site. Then nothing until two weeks ago when she starts logging onto a games forum."

"In Japan."

"Right. In Japan. Some sort of online RPG thing. I can get you a rough address."

"Is this games thing in Japanese?"

"Yeah."

Blaine sighed. "KT, I seriously doubt our girl speaks Japanese."

KT started to get huffy. "Look, you asked me to trace the laptop, not the girl. And all right, I might've got a bit overexcited, but I have. So I want paying, okay?"

"Don't worry I'm gonna pay you. It's just… it's entirely possible the computer was nicked over here and then sold off, right?"

"It's possible," KT said slowly, "but I don't know why anyone would bother. This laptop ain't exactly a great piece of kit, you know what I mean? I don't see why if it was nicked over here it wouldn't be sold here too. Why would anyone go to all the trouble of shipping it to Asia?"

"Why would she go to Japan? *How* would she get there?"

"That's your problem, not mine. I'm just saying the thing's over there and I reckon the most likely explanation is that she took it."

"She didn't even take her passport with her when she disappeared."

"So? It's not impossible she got abroad without one. Maybe she bought a fake one."

"A fake passport! They don't exactly grow on trees."

"Look, whatever, I don't know. All I can tell you is that the computer is definitely there."

"All right, thanks." Blaine sighed. "Email me the details and I'll send you some cash. Call me if you find out anything else." He hung up and went back to sleep.

He slept for another four hours and had just climbed out of bed to have a shower when his mobile rang again.

"Hello?"

"Blaine - you bastard! You could've told me there's a warrant out for this girl."

Blaine shifted the phone under his chin. "Sorry Peirce," he said. "I didn't know." He'd suspected there might be – Faber had said she was a killer – but he hadn't known for sure.

Silence. "Yeah, right. You just didn't think I'd do it if I knew the file was hot. Don't pull that shit on me again. You're not exactly still in the force. If I'd tripped something getting it for you -"

"I'm sorry. I really am."

"Humph." Sounding only slightly mollified, Peirce continued his rant. "*And* you could've told me she's the daughter of a celebrity."

"What?"

"She's Robert Eury's daughter!"

"Who's he?" Blaine remembered his name from the books in Bunny's flat.

Peirce took a deep breath. "Have you done any research on this case at all?"

"I got it ten minutes before I called you."

"Jesus." There was a muffled sound and Blaine imagined his friend swapping the receiver from one ear to the other in exasperation. "Right. Robert Eury is famous in academic circles. Seriously, he's like a god to some people. He's one hot-shit hardcore philosopher."

Blaine found himself laughing. "A hardcore philosopher?"

"Hey, I took a course in it at uni. It's fucking deep. You don't mess with it."

"All right, okay. So what's he famous for?"

"Loads of stuff. It's all in the murder file. He's written tons of books and I think I've even read one of them. I think it was called *Emerging From Materialism*."

"Okay, great. Could you email me all this stuff, plus anything else that looks relevant? Is there anything else I urgently need to know?"

"Only that the girl's pretty hot for it, the fact the murder weapon turned up in her flat is pretty conclusive. And she's set to inherit everything – the old man had clearly been saving his pennies – the house and nearly two hundred thousand cash."

"Wait... hot for what? What is it she's wanted for?"

"You don't even know *that*?"

"No?"

"She's wanted for homicide. She's wanted for murdering her father."

After the unsettling telephone call Blaine got in the shower and then went downstairs for breakfast. After his Full English he came back into his room and plugged his laptop into the hotel's wireless system. Upon checking his emails he discovered he had four new messages in his Inbox but only two of them were of any interest: one from KT and one from Peirce. KT's email was short and just contained the address he'd traced Bunny's laptop to in Japan. In contrast Peirce's email proved a treasure trove of information. It contained just three words in the message body - 'Here ya go' – but the attachments were priceless. Blaine sorted them into three distinct groups: excerpts from newspaper cuttings, the murder file and the missing persons file.

He began with the newspaper cuttings. The first was a copy of *The Times* obituary for 18th August. Underneath a sombre headline - 'Famous academic Robert Eury murdered' - lay the following story:

'Three days ago Professor Robert Benjamin Eury was found murdered in his home village of Pottersby. A local pensioner, a Mrs Josephine Garmin, came across the body in a disused forest chapel while walking her dog. She then returned to her home and called the police forthwith, who arrived nearly an hour later. The police have released no details of the death except to confirm that it is being looked at as a murder case. They are currently searching for Eury's next-of-kin: his daughter Beatrice has been missing for two days.

'The circumstances of Eury's death aside, his life should be celebrated as befits one of such academic fame and eccentric notoriety. Eury was born on 6th June 1943 in Dorset. He graduated with a MA in Philosophy from the University of Edinburgh in 1963 and subsequently studied for a BPhil and then a DPhil in Philosophy at St Catherine's College, Oxford. Eury specialised in Metaphysics and Philosophy of Mind early on his career and taught at Kings College, London before eventually attaining a Chair at St Stephen's College, Oxford in 1974. He achieved academic fame in the late sixties with his book On Necessary Physicalism *and afterwards went on to produce dozens of other academic works. After the death of his wife in 1987 Eury retired from teaching and moved to the hamlet of Pottersby just outside Shropshire. He continued to*

publish right up until his death.'

The scanned article cut off here – perhaps Peirce had thought the rest wasn't worth reading. The other newspaper clip was taken from *The Sun* on 19th August and was headed with a garish banner: 'Professor hung, drawn and quartered'. It told how Professor Eury had been stabbed six times in the chest and then hung sometime after death. It revealed that Miss Beatrice Eury was now a suspect in her father's murder.

The copy of the open police murder file held more detail. Blaine read on, becoming engrossed in the tale of patricide. Eury had been murdered at some time on 15th August. He'd been stabbed through the heart with a bread knife. His body was discovered on 17th August and when the police tried to contact his daughter as next-of-kin it was found that she had not gone to work the day before. She had not in fact been seen since leaving work on the afternoon of 15th August. A search of her flat yielded the murder weapon and Bunny was officially declared a suspect. The motive for the killing was unclear but as she would receive a modest inheritance the most probable one seemed to be money. The fact she'd gone missing only confirmed her guilt. Once the murder weapon had been found at her apartment a nation-wide search had been launched for her arrest but she had not been found.

The missing persons file had been linked to the homicide file and it contained little new information except for its short biography. Beatrice Amelia Eury had been born on 16th February 1981 in Oxford to Professor Robert Eury and his wife Mary. At four years old her mother had died and she'd been moved to Pottersby. Bunny had been home-educated until she eleven – Blaine wondered at that until he saw the distance Pottersby lay from the nearest town – and after secondary school studied at the University of Warwick. She was currently employed by St John's Primary School in Lowestoft as a Year Five teacher. She had many friends but no steady boyfriend. Her flat was rented on a year-long lease. Since her disappearance her car and laptop had not been found. Her passport and credit card had been left behind in Lowestoft. The feeling in the file seemed to be that she was dead and the body simply hadn't turned up yet. It was unlikely that she had been on the run for ten weeks and survived.

Attached to the missing persons file were copies of Bunny's debit and credit card statements. Blaine studied them curiously. She wasn't in debt but she was hardly rich either – on 16th August she'd had exactly £2,157.02 in her HSBC current account. She didn't have a savings account. There was £102.38 outstanding on her MasterCard but nothing that wouldn't have been paid off by her monthly direct debit. Nothing on her phone bill stood out either. The only item of interest was the fact she'd withdrawn £2,000 in cash from the small HSBC branch in Ellesmere at 3:18pm the day after the murder. That two grand raised some possibilities: it might not be enough to go on the run for over two months with but it could certainly provide a head-start. It could buy you several weeks in a cheap hostel, a ferry ticket to France or a plane ticket to anywhere. Blaine wanted to dismiss the idea she'd left the country, because she'd left her passport behind, but the possibility nagged at him. The information uncovered by KT was tantalising as well as potentially useless – if she *had* left the country finding her would be much harder.

Blaine sighed when he finished reading and sat back on the double bed. What to do next? It was now 10:15am and if he was going to check out of the Swan Hotel he needed to leave by midday.

He tried to consider the likeliest explanations for her disappearance. The first was the one the police had raised: Bunny hadn't been found because she was dead. Perhaps after the murder she'd trekked deep into the forest and killed herself. She could have dumped her car or hidden it in the woods. But then why bother to get the cash? Perhaps she had gone on the run for a little while and then died. If this were the case it was unlikely that Blaine would ever find her and he wasn't sure Faber would pay him anything for discovering her body. The second possibility was that she was on the run and had simply got damn good at it over the last ten weeks. That would mean she could be anywhere in the country, perhaps still hiding out in the woods or working in a town that didn't ask too many questions. Blaine scrubbed his hands through his hair, messing up the black locks even more than they were before. He could follow the standard procedures for both of those possibilities easily: go to the scene of the murder, do some hiking around Bayleir Forest, interview her friends and work colleagues to see if there were any distant relatives she might have run to. The problem with following those standard procedures was that they'd already been followed by numerous people before him. Not only had the police been chasing her but he had no doubt that Faber had hired other private investigators – perhaps even professional hitmen – to find Bunny before contacting him. The scientist's approach to O'Dwyer Investigations and his bizarre offer was the last resort of a desperate man. But the police and Faber's other investigators had all failed.

So what could Blaine do to find Bunny that the police and the other investigators hadn't? He found himself looking down at the notebook on his bedside table, with the words 'RPG gaming – Tokyo' scribbled on them.

Surely that was madness. But it was undeniably a lead that nobody else had uncovered. Nobody else had access to a hacker as good as KT. Blaine stretched out on the bed covers and stared up at the smoothly plastered ceiling, trying to think outside the box. Eventually he sat up and began doodling on his notepad. He wrote down three phrases beside the first and linked them in a sort of mind map: 'missing laptop', 'missing car', '£2,000 cash'. Putting aside for one moment the fact she didn't have a passport, she would have had enough money to buy a plane ticket. Where could she have gone? Blaine lightly circled the word 'Tokyo'.

With a frown he turned back to his laptop and logged onto Expedia. Twenty minutes later he had established that Heathrow was the only UK airport with a direct link to Japan. Of course, it was possible that she hadn't flown direct, that she'd been country-skipping for some time… but she didn't have much money and Blaine was willing to bet that if she was using a fake passport she'd only want to risk it once. Very gently he drew a circle around all the words on his notepad and bit the tip of his pen. There was only one thing left that didn't fit… what had she done with her car? With an even deeper frown he went online again and found a telephone number for Heathrow airport parking services.

"Hi, I have a car that I'd like to leave at the airport in long term parking while I'm away on business. I'd like to know how long I can it leave it for, how much it costs, et cetera."

"Well," said the bored serviceman, "you can leave it as long as you like, but it's £15.40 for the first three days and £14.90 for every day after that so we rarely get cars parked for more than a few weeks."

"But I could leave it a few months if I needed to?"

"Yeah, sure, if you're happy to pay for it."

"Okay, thanks. Out of interest, how many cars do you have in your long term parking?"

"Thousands, mate."

"All right, cheers, you've been really helpful." Blaine hung up.

He checked his watch and it was nearing 11:00am. He could stay and do the sensible thing – interview Bunny's work colleagues – or he could follow the crazy idea taking shape on his notepad. Ten minutes later Blaine was back in his Rover, heading towards Heathrow.

The drive back to London was slow due to heavy traffic and by the time he arrived at Heathrow Airport it was mid-afternoon. Blaine parked his car in short term parking and then made his way around to long term parking, a good fifteen minute walk away. When he arrived Blaine sauntered over to the two security guards sitting in a ticket booth. He tried to appear as friendly and harmless as possible.

"Hi there," Blaine smiled and even gave a little wave. "I know this is a bit random, but I was wondering if I could get something out of my friend's car. It's parked in one of the long-term parking bays."

"Why?" said the younger guard, suspiciously. He was wearing a baseball cap over his uniform and had terrible acne.

"My friend left her address book in it but she's in the States for at least another fortnight and she's beginning to panic about not having it. I live in London so she asked if I could come get it."

The teenager opened his mouth to speak but the other guard, a middle aged man, interrupted him. "Have you got the keys, son?"

"Right here." Blaine jangled his car keys.

"All right, then. I can't see the harm in it." The older guard leaned over the computer terminal in the guard shack. "What's her name?"

"B. Eury."

There was silence except for the man's laborious, index finger typing. "There's no B. Eury. Just an A. Eury."

"Ah, she must've used her middle name." Blaine tried to sound nonchalant when inwardly his excitement was rising. She'd been clever enough to hide her car in a forest of cars but not to use a fake name! "Just to check it's the right one… she put it in on the 16th August, right? Paid cash?"

"Yeah, that's it." The guard smiled and gestured Blaine towards the north car park. "It's in Bay 28, Lot 43. I hope you find the book."

"Thanks."

As Blaine strolled out amongst the thousands of cars he felt like whistling. It was a chilly November day – the British winter was definitely coming – but the sun still shone weakly through the clouds. The light reflected off the myriad sheets of painted metal and Blaine actually wished he'd brought sunglasses. The parking bays were completely deserted; they reminded Blaine of a scene in Stephen King's *The Stand* where the characters enter a deserted turnpike filled with cars, the drivers either overtaken by plague or fled. The field of metal seemed desolate, alien somehow. He was glad to finally arrive in Bay 28, Lot 43 of this machine jungle. And there, sitting like some lost treasure in the wilderness, was Bunny's blue Mini. Just to be sure Blaine got out his notebook and checked that the licence plate – S364 DWT – was correct. It was. Even if Bunny had paid for three months parking she'd still have had enough money left over to buy a plane ticket. Smiling to himself Blaine knelt down by the driver's side and pulled out his lock picking kit.

Twenty minutes later he'd gone through the contents of the car: a novel by Douglas Coupland, several crumpled petrol receipts, a blue polka-dot umbrella, a fawn raincoat and – most tantalisingly – a pair of size five kitten heels coated in mud and leaf mush. Blaine took several photos of the car and its contents on his mobile then headed back towards his own vehicle. When he passed the security booth he took his notebook out of his pocket and gave them a wave with it. The older guard waved back and the young one sulked on.

Back in his car Blaine called Faber on the private number he'd been given.

The phone rang seven times before it was picked up. "Faber speaking."

"Hi, it's Blaine. I have some news."

"One moment please." There were some muffled sounds and Blaine imagined Faber leaving some important board meeting so he could talk in privacy. "You can go ahead now."

"I've made some progress. I've found her car."

"Really?" There was no mistaking the excitement in the doctor's voice.

"Yeah. I've also traced her laptop. Her car is parked at Heathrow Airport and her laptop is in Japan."

There was a sharp hiss of indrawn breath down the line and it began to drizzle outside. Blaine half-turned the key in the ignition and switched his windscreen wipers on.

"Japan..." Faber sounded as though he was tasting the word. He sounded surprised but there was another note there, too.

"Yeah. Obviously it's unlikely that she's there – I don't see how she could have got there without a passport – but when I go to Pottersby I'm going to see if her father had any links to Japan. Perhaps if I could find out how the laptop left the country I could find where she is."

"Pottersby?" Faber's voice became angry and harsh.

The sudden change reminded Blaine of Lilly – her mood changes could be as shocking as that. Cruel and capricious like the sea.

"Now I know about the murder I want to go and visit the site. I know it's been nearly three months since she went missing but that's still the freshest trail."

A pause. "There is nothing in Pottersby. You will not go there to look for her."

Blaine was bewildered by the fierceness in Faber's tone. "Okay. Then what would you like me to do?"

There was another long pause, and the drizzle outside the car intensified. Blaine watched his reflection in the windscreen, a pale blob with a machine glued to his ear. When Faber didn't reply Blaine spoke again. "What *is* it you'd like me to do? I could hand over to you what I've found, you could hire someone else in Japan or give it to the authorities."

"No." Short and sharp. "I've had people looking for this girl for months and you're the first one to actually come up with anything. Nothing's changed. I want you to go to Japan and do as we originally agreed."

Blaine jerked up in his seat. "Go to Japan? That's pretty far out of our original agreement! I don't speak Japanese and this whole thing is probably a wild goose chase. I won't exactly be inconspicuous over there, either."

"Is money the problem? I'll give you an advance on the half million. Obviously I'd pay your expenses."

Blaine shut his eyes and sucked in some air. "Well, okay. I guess I'll go. But even if you give me an advance I can't promise anything. She may never have been to Tokyo and even if she was there she could be somewhere else by now."

"No, she's there." Faber said slowly. "In fact it makes an odd sort of sense. Book yourself on the next flight out." The line went dead.

Blaine sat in his car for five minutes afterwards, holding his phone and gazing out at the grey rain coating his windscreen.

Ten hours later he was sitting in the First Class compartment of a British Airways night-flight to Tokyo, with a whiskey in his right hand and a *Lonely Planet* guide on his lap. There had been no time to go home and pack – what he didn't already have with him he'd bought in Departures. The only real problem was that he'd had to leave his guns in the back of his car but he doubted that Faber would mind the expense of replacing them.

Blaine reclined in his wide, soft chair and looked out of the porthole-style window. First Class seats always reminded him slightly of cocoons: they suggested that with the minimum of tubing they could be upgraded to feed you and take away your waste. He'd wanted to be an astronaut as a kid – what boy didn't? – and as an adult he realised that this was the closest he'd ever get. The flight would be twelve hours long and he knew it would make sense to get some sleep but for now he was too wired. How the hell had he got into this mess? He knew very little about Japan and didn't like sushi. What he did know of the country came mainly through pop culture: *Memoirs of a Geisha*, futuristic technologies, Hello Kitty, Sony games consoles, manga films… and of course that old HSBC advert featuring a businessman eating eels because he didn't know it was impolite in Japanese culture to completely clear your plate. As a solider Blaine also knew a little about their military history: their actions in the two world wars, the Nanjing massacre and Hiroshima. The most recent thing he knew about Japan was the terrible Valentine's Day earthquake; on the afternoon of 14th February a huge quake had rocked Tokyo. It had resulted in mammoth fires and explosions, flooring a whole set of skyscrapers. Several thousand people had been killed but luckily the quake had been extremely localised and the damage well contained. As far as Blaine knew the area was still being rebuilt, a huge scar of concrete rubble somewhere in the city. He remembered that after the horrific event a BBC news reporter had compared it to an apocalyptic scene in the famous film *Akira* and in the wake of the controversy the reporter lost his position. Blaine hoped that no more earthquakes were in the offing and that he'd be able to complete his job quickly. With a sigh he reclined into his cocoon and opened the guidebook.

Ten hours later Blaine awoke with the book on his chest and rubbed his eyes clear of sleep. The plane's interior lights were dimmed and he pushed up the plastic screen that lay over his window. The sky was completely black outside and as a cloud drifted out of his line of sight he saw thousands of diamond-like stars glittering in the velvet firmament. All was quiet in the world as he sat there, taking in that vast darkness. After a few minutes he caught sight of his stubbly jaw in the glass and turned away. He dozed a little more and then was awakened as the plane prepared for landing. Leaning towards the window again, Blaine saw that they had dipped below cloud cover and realised that the multitude of stars beneath him were actually the lights of Tokyo shining out into the night. Unlike the actual stars there was some order to the lights below - they reminded Blaine of a documentary he'd once seen about the life that existed in the mostly uncharted deeps of the ocean. Down in those green abyss existed spirals of glimmering algae, gleaming dotted lines cast out from central points into star-shapes and ovals. The tiny structures had shone from the inky waves like underwater stars. Blaine put his fingertips against the window and stared at the sunken city.
From far below something in the city stared up at him.

Shortly after those detached, silent moments Blaine found himself in the noisy bustle of baggage claim. Blaine had left Heathrow at 11:00pm on Thursday and although the flight had only taken twelve hours it was now 7:00pm on Friday, because Tokyo was eight hours ahead of London. He'd effectively lost a day. As he stood in line around the baggage reel the whole experience was beginning to feel more and more surreal. To distract himself he tried to put himself in Bunny's shoes – what would she have done when she'd arrived here? She'd probably want to hole up somewhere... somewhere cheap. Her supply of cash must have been almost gone. A hostel then? No... there would be backpackers there and they'd be sociable types. She'd want to avoid Westerners. Perhaps a cheap hotel? That sounded more likely. Blaine sighed and tiredly scrubbed his sore head. By the time he'd grabbed his bag from the conveyor and hoisted it over his right shoulder he'd already decided to pick a low-range hotel from the *Lonely Planet*.

As Blaine stepped out of baggage reclaim and into the queue for Passport Control he was already beginning to feel out of place. There were a few other Caucasians standing in line but not many and Blaine felt as though he was towering over everyone. He had certainly been right when he'd told Faber he'd be too conspicuous in this country. He could only hope that would apply to Bunny, too. It would make her easier to find. Once he'd cleared Passport Control he walked into Arrivals and only then did he begin to grasp the scale of Tokyo airport. Thousands of people bustled around him and he was pushed forwards and backwards around suitcases, crates on metal wheelies and families holding hands with their children. The din was bewildering, music and language that Blaine didn't understand blared at him from all directions and a group of young children rushed up to shout unknown phrases at his knees.

"*Konnichi wa!*"

"*Mite goran! Mite goran!*"

Blaine motioned them away and retreated to a far, high wall near a cash point to try and take his bearings. In the previous parts of the airport signs had been in English as well in Japanese but now everything was only written in the square Japanese characters. Blaine had never really travelled outside of his tours in the Army. His eyes darted around him, a bitter taste in his mouth as adrenalin and jet-lag kicked in. Being so totally alone in a foreign country was exhilarating and scary.

Taking control of himself, Blaine wandered over to the huge sets of revolving doors that led outside. As soon as he left the air conditioned building the humidity hit him like a wall. Even though it was dark outside clouds hung low over the city. Blaine made his way towards a row of cars that looked like a taxi rank. He pointed to the name of the hotel he'd picked in his guidebook (helpfully, it was printed in both Japanese and English) and then rubbed his thumb and forefinger together. The taxi driver pulled a calculator out of his breast pocket and typed in a price. Blaine shook his head and pointed to the amount written in the *Lonely Planet*. The driver shook his head and typed a price somewhere in the middle of the previous two. Blaine smiled and nodded his head. The driver held open the door for him and Blaine got into the car.

As the driver set off Blaine got his first good look at Tokyo. It had taken him nearly an hour to get out of the airport and it was now 8:00pm but the city showed no sign of cooling down for the day. There was lots of traffic on the roads and hundreds of pedestrians on the pavements. At first the taxi seemed to be driving through a concrete maze; the tall walls that rose up on either side of the road were plastered with toothpaste ads and pictures of cars. There was a lot of graffiti, swirling characters in purple and neon yellow. Everything was covered with the flowing, hieroglyphic-like Japanese characters. They reminded Blaine a little of the heavily stylised calligraphy produced by monks in centuries past. After twenty minutes of driving they pulled up out of the concrete gorges and the road rose up onto a hill from where they could look down on the city. Tall buildings, concrete boxes and glistening skyscrapers stretched out in all directions as far as the eye could see. Everything had an oriental twist to it; the roofs were oddly shaped and the drain pipes were decorative. Asian faces crowded the pavements and many of the slim Japanese women in their smart suits boasted the smooth, shining black hair that they were famed for. The taxi whizzed on, navigating the alien roads with their strange streets signs effortlessly. Blaine vowed to himself not to rent a car here. As they entered the city proper the panoramic views faded and the cab began to drive deeper into the twisting streets, in between the rows of buildings. The taxi wound its way through shops and restaurants, no longer through offices and warehouses. Although the buildings were still hugely tall – they must all have at least twenty stories – they weren't made of shining glass any more but were rather huge constructs of steel and cement. Windows were everywhere and streetlamps reflected lazily off all the glass. Eventually the driver took a left turn into a set of much smaller alleys and pointed to a building as he ground to a halt.

Prepared for this, Blaine compared the characters in his guide book to those over the door of the indicated building – they did seem to proclaim that this was the Aki Hotel - and nodded. He paid the driver in Yen he'd picked up at Heathrow and slid out of the cab. The hotel seemed to be surrounded by shops, cafes and residential buildings. He entered the hotel slowly, taking in everything around him. The door was open and the hallway inside was filled with posters depicting mountains. Blaine assumed they were Japanese mountain ranges. At the end of the corridor there were some stairs and what looked like a reception desk. Blaine rang the bell on the wooden sill and after a few minutes a harassed-looking woman appeared.

"Hi," he said slowly. "I'm looking for a room?"

The lady replied with a flood of Japanese and then, after some rummaging, produced a card with the following printed on it: 'Single – ¥14,000. Double – ¥18,500. Single + bathroom – ¥23,000. Double + bathroom – ¥29,000'. Blaine pointed to the third option on the list and handed over enough money for four nights. The woman nodded and after more rummaging produced a set of keys.

Blaine turned to go up the stairs but this prompted another stream of Japanese and the woman tapped the wall on the right side of her desk. Blaine belatedly saw that there was a lift there, recessed into an alcove. The woman pushed a button, then used one of the keys. She did it all with much pointing, so that Blaine understood he was meant to study this for future reference. After ten seconds or so the lift doors rumbled open and with more pointing the lady pushed a button labelled '17'. The two of them stepped inside and as the lift rose creakily upwards Blaine became aware of how short the woman was. She barely came up to his chest and Blaine's hair brushed the ceiling of the elevator. He felt awkward, oversized and slightly claustrophobic. The woman's heavy, musky perfume didn't help.

Eventually the lift creaked to a halt and the woman stepped out, mumbling to herself. Blaine found himself in a dimly-lit corridor lined with doors, and wondered if the hotel occupied all of the building's floors or just a few of them. Surely it could only be some of them – wouldn't a bigger hotel have a nicer reception area? As the woman led him down the corridor he noticed that her tight bun was held in place with a biro. She turned into the third door on the left, marked '210', and pointedly handed Blaine two keys. He used the one that hadn't been used on the lift and the door *snicked* open. The lady clapped delightedly, the smile on her face changing the directions of the lines on her skin, and switched the light on inside the room before hurrying off. Blaine waved goodbye but her back was already turned. With a shrug he went into the room and shut the door behind him.

The room was tiny - it looked as if it had been built around the double bed that was squeezed against three of its walls. Blaine thought he'd asked for a single bedroom and then thought that perhaps a double bedroom just gave you, literally, more room. There was a gap a few feet wide between the foot of the bed and fourth wall and on the right side, in the corner, was a slim door that led to the bathroom. In the small amount of space at the foot of the bed was a tall, thin chest of drawers with a TV and a vase of flowers on top. When Blaine investigated the bathroom he found that it was about the size of an up-ended coffin. It was actually a wet room: the whole thing was lined in rubber and it was so small it would be possible to have a shower, sit on the toilet and wash your hands in the sink all at the same time. With a sigh he threw his bag down on the bed and stripped off for a shower. By the time he'd towelled himself down it was nearly 9:00pm and he felt desperately tired. Even though he knew it wouldn't help his jetlag he climbed into bed, drew the curtains above the headboard and set the alarm on his mobile to wake in him an hour so that he could have a quick nap.

As he slept something searched for him.

CHAPTER 4

Stories are often preoccupied with beginnings.

For Bunny, we have seen that the story began one hot day in August when she found her father's body swinging in the woods. We have seen that for Blaine the story began when he met with Dr Faber and agreed to kill another woman for money (although, in truth, Blaine's feet were set on that path over three years ago). But are either of those points *really* the beginning of this story?

No.

This story doesn't begin with either of them. Blaine and Bunny are merely caught pieces of flotsam, collateral wisps of seaweed that have been tossed up by foamy tides and pulled back down into the ocean's depths.

If there is a specific beginning to this story, to which an omniscient narrator could point and whisper *'There'*, it would at the birth of a little boy named Chiko Tentori. Chiko is four years old, a beautiful kid with a shock of thick black hair and brown eyes. To understand a little more about him we're going to rewind the tape, go back in time to February.

We're going to start the tape on 7th February and go back to the happiest memory Chiko has. His parents have taken him by train all the way north to Sapporo, for the Japanese Snow Festival.

February is a good month to live in Japan. The city of Sapporo is blanketed under white sheets of snow, its curving roofs and domes rendered frostily beautiful. It's still deep winter and there are as yet no fluffy blossoms hanging on trees but red berries can be seen poking out from underneath icy branches. On the morning of the first day of the festival Chiko could be found standing straight up and pressed against the large windows of his hotel room, his hands and forehead resting on the cold glass. He mouth was open in a huge smile.

The Sapporo Snow Festival is a beautiful event - a time where artists come from all over the country to craft sculptures in ice and snow. Chiko had recently celebrated his fourth birthday, and was desperately excited to be taken by his loving parents away from his home in Tokyo to see these icy exhibits. His parents had bundled them all up in heavy winter coats, gloves and hats and had taken him into the city centre on the bus. Chiko also loved the bus, loved looking at the curious people that rode on it. His excitement had quite erased from his mind the barrage of medical tests he'd taken two days before – MRI scans and yet more blood tests. The doctors hadn't figured out what was wrong with him yet but the latest in a long line of specialists seemed to be doing a little more than the others. The most recent doctor was building a new machine – especially for him – to try and understand his condition. The machine was formed entirely of sleek silver curves and had lots of pretty wires hanging out of it; it wasn't yet finished though and the doctor would often wire Chiko up to it in order to perfect it further. Chiko liked playing with the pieces of wire, all tangled up like multi-coloured lengths of wool. His parents had faith that they would diagnose their little boy's problem soon and Chiko was glad that they were less worried about him. But Chiko wasn't going to think about any of that today.

When the bus arrived in the city centre and his parents helped him off he hopped along beside them down the crunchy white pavement to the entrance to Odori Park. His father paid the entrance fee and then... then they were inside the Snow Festival. To the little boy it was a winter wonderland of delight, a magical place. Snow was falling gently onto the ground as he and his parents trudged through the park; the sun was shining faintly through the fluffy clouds and it was very cold. Chiko's mother held one of his mittened hands as she and his father led him around ice sculptures of elephants, flowers and castles. There was plenty of room to move around the exhibits in the park and as they walked Chiko's boots crunched in the frosty grass. There was one section devoted to a group of artists from China, who had crafted huge ice sculptures of flowers and filled them with lanterns. Little yellow lights glowed from deep within their frosty curves. The other families around them 'ooh-ed' and 'ah-ed' – the universal language of wonder. Occasionally Chiko would see something he really liked and would tug on his mother's coat sleeve: *"Okassan..."*

The best sculpture of all was a dragon. It was built half under and around some fir trees and rose to the size of a hippo. It was shaped out of ice with a large neck, four taloned feet and a great curling tail that wound around the tree. The whole dragon was oriental in style, from the many tendrils springing from its backbone to its long eyelashes. The head came up to the shoulders of Chiko's father and the little boy liked to stand under its jaws and look up into the eyes of the dragon. There were inches to spare between the start of the creature's icy beard and Chiko's mop of soft black hair. Chiko's parents laughed to see their son standing straight, his head craned back as far as it would go, staring into the dragon's crystalline bulbous eyes. Chiko would take a deep breath, puffing his chest out as far as he could, then blow out in a huge exhalation so that his cheeks were rosy and his breath frosted in the air like dragon steam.

The next night, after his parents had taken him by train back to their middle-class home in Tokyo, they stayed up late after putting Chiko to bed and whispered about him in their bedroom. None of the doctors seemed to know what to do… should they spend more money on specialists or just hope it was some sort of stage that would pass? Chiko's parents loved him very much but they were well out of their depth.

And, unbeknownst to his parents, Chiko had slipped out of his bed and padded across the lounge to make his dragon breath appear on the large windows. The little boy placed his palms flat against the dark glass, his fingertips pushing against the cold surface. Outside rain swirled and splattered against the windowpane, the occasional individual drop outlined like a firefly in the neon signs that clung to the outside of the building. The apartment was on the fourteenth floor of a tall building; the street that the boy was looking down into seemed far away. Skyscrapers glittered on the horizon, moving lights from cars and streetlamps dotted the entire city even though it was near midnight. Tokyo never slept.

Chiko knew that he should have been sleeping. He was a slight child, with smooth skin and chocolate-brown eyes. As his eyes tracked the movements in the city below his mouth hung slightly open and the tip of one front tooth protruded. He had lost two other milk teeth just a few days ago. He was wrapped up in bright blue pyjamas and his thick hair was unruly from lying in bed. He had sneaked out of his bedroom once he'd heard his parents retire; they would never have knowingly let him stay up so late. But Chiko loved this view too much to be denied it: night after night he crept out of his bed and came to this window to look down on the city. He shut his eyes and pressed his hands harder against the window, imagining that he could push though it and turn into a dragon so that he could fly through the darkness and carve twisting flight-paths around the lights.

Beneath Chiko's fingertips, the glass began to bulge.

Having explained a little more about Chiko we will fast-forward to the day of the Valentine Earthquake. It occurred seven days after Chiko had been taken to the Snow Festival, on that day that Chiko and his parents were riding the subway back to their home in the district of Takanosu from a shopping trip. They were seated in happy silence in the carriage when the train began to shudder. It was still very cold and everyone in the carriage was wearing rain gear with slippery shoes and cagoules. The quake felt like an explosion and the *boomph* as it slapped through the cabin threw the world into chaos.

People screamed as the train rocked off its rails, everyone was jerked suddenly as it crashed onto its side. Hats and bags went flying, smoke and dust filled the compartment. Chiko's eyes and mouth became clogged with dust, his eyes were watering and all he could see were the thick grey particles hanging in the air all around him. The explosion had effectively stuffed cotton wool in his ears and he could hear only a little above the ringing in his head; he tried to reach for his parents but failed to touch anything as he instead bounced around in the soft, thick air. He could hear shouting and the angry *beeps* of alarms going off but they were all muffled, all far away. The world he found himself in was dark and grey, like he'd suddenly been transported into the centre of one of those glass balls filled with white flecks that you shook to make a snowstorm. Chiko wiped at his eyes some more and wished, as instinctively as any child, to be somewhere safe and dark and far away from the frightening motion. He succumbed a moment later to an unconsciousness as deep as death.

The Valentine's Earthquake was unusual in several ways. Unlike most earthquakes it produced no seismic activity at all in the hours preceding the event and there was no aftershock. This actually prompted some scientists to claim that the destruction was the result of a bomb rather than heated geological activity but there was no evidence other than the unusual nature of the quake to support their claim. This led to a stream of academic papers a little later in the year, with some scientists arguing that the event was just an unusual geological blip and others arguing that it was either triggered by, or the result of, manmade explosives. As it happens, scientists on both sides of the debate were wrong.

Unaware of the cause of the subway explosion, Chiko awoke coughing into thick darkness. He opened his eyes but could see nothing and they still stung with dust. He put his hands out and felt a hard, crumbly surface beneath them. He felt around his body and sat up when he felt nothing threatening. He tried to call out but dust and grit choked his throat and he doubled over in a coughing fit. He had no idea where he was or how he'd arrived there but even his child's mind realised he couldn't stay where he was.

Chiko pushed himself to his feet and took a few stumbling steps forwards, his arms stretched out in front of him. After only two of those zombie-steps he tripped over something lying on the ground. Chiko landed heavily, grazing his palms, and he let out a short muffled cry that precipitated another coughing fit. He tried hard not to cry and instead fumbled his hands over the object lying in his path. It was a hard, cloth-covered bundle that seemed to have straps. Chiko yowled with delight – he'd found his backpack! His little fingers reached for the zippers and unfastened the front compartment. He slid his bottle of Coke out from the pocket and took a long swig. The sugary drink soothed his throat and he felt stronger. Chiko stood up again and started to walk.

Before long he'd established that he was in a tunnel of some sort – walls ran roughly parallel on either side of him and he could go in either direction. Chiko placed his left hand on one wall and took that direction at random. He walked for a timeless interval; his Pokémon watch had broken in the subway accident and although the dial glowed green the hands failed to move. His backpack grew heavier on its straps and Chiko was considering stopping for a rest when the air suddenly seemed to clear and his eyes detected a faint illumination up ahead. Chiko broke into a run, hungry for light. As he ran his surroundings revealed themselves: the walls, ceilings and floor were made of concrete, twisted girders and dry brown earth. Sometimes the ceilings disappeared completely and Chiko could look up and see wide-open spaces filled with glinting, criss-crossing beams and wooden rafters. He was in a forgotten place under the city. He slowed to a walk and began to understand that the light came not from daylight but from electronic lights buried somewhere beneath the surface that somehow filtered down to this place deep underground. As he slowed he heard a mewling noise like a trapped kitten and he turned around in a circle to search for it.

The tunnel widened out a bit here and this was one of the places where the ceiling had collapsed in a shower of stone and mud to the floor. Above the little boy was a tall shadowy space punctuated by broken girders and small rays of grey light. One of the rock falls looked relatively recent – dust was still dancing around the piles of bricks and earth – and when Chiko moved towards it he found the source of the mewing.

Another boy was caught there under the rubble, his right arm and leg buried under crumbling stone. He looked about the same age as Chiko, his hair was slightly longer and thinner, but they could have passed for brothers. His eyes widened when he saw Chiko and he paused in his crying to reach out his free hand for help. Chiko ran forward and tried to free him from the debris, moving small rocks with his hands and kicking at the larger pieces of earth.

"Daijoobu desu, yoroshii desu, ii desu!" Chiko kept shouting in reassurance, and suddenly between them the boy's arm came free. It was bent at an awkward angle and the boy went pale when he saw it but helped Chiko uncover his leg anyway. Before long his whole body was free of the stone and the boy hugged Chiko hard.

"What's your name?" The boy asked in Japanese.

"Chiko Tentori."

"I'm Akifumi." They shook hands and a firm friendship was formed.

The two of them wandered on together after that, holding hands and chatting to keep the darkness at bay. Akifumi had been in the basement of his apartment building when it collapsed, he said that he had fallen down a chute-like crack in the floor into a tunnel that smelled like a toilet and then that too had cracked and he had somehow ended up here. Chiko in turn told him about how he'd escaped the ruined subway train.

The pair walked on through the bowels of the city well into the night, although as the light never changed and as neither had a working watch they had no way of knowing it. Nothing changed until the tunnel widened out again into a low pit – what little light came from above was already receding – and they heard voices somewhere in the distance. Akifumi's brown eyes widened and he gripped Chiko's hand harder as a group of young boys emerged from the broken walls and piles of earth at the end of the tunnel. The pair stood silent and motionless together as the other children surrounded them. The boys wore rags and their hair was long and unkempt, they looked fierce and thin.

"Who are you?" The tallest boy asked.

"We came in the earthquake," Chiko said.

The tall boy shrugged. "Okay." He turned away and that seemed to be it.

Chiko, Akifumi and another boy named Taisuke had all come from the earthquake that day. They were accepted by the street children with indifference. They learned quickly how to go up to the surface to steal, how to make cooking fires where the smoke could rise high away and how to obey the complicated net of superstitions the group ascribed to the city.

Chiko learnt of the existence of the *Tokai-Kaibutsu* four days after he arrived in the home of the street children. There were about a dozen children crowded round a large fire they'd lit underground and the smoke curled upwards into one of the airy spaces in the foundations of the city above. One of the other boys had made a comment about the *Tokai-Kaibutsu* and Akifumi had asked what it was.

"You've never heard of the Tokai-Kaibutsu?" The older boy seemed genuinely amazed.

"I've never heard of it either," said Chiko.

"Ah." The older boy gestured to another, smaller boy on the far side of the fire. "Yasunobu, tell us the story of the *Tokai-Kaibutsu*."

So Yasunobu moved forward and told the story of the *Tokai-Kaibutsu* while everyone huddled up in their blankets.

"The *Tokai-Kaibutsu*," Yasunobu explained, "is the spirit of the city. It is a great beast, like a tiger or a dragon, made of the air we breathe and the bricks around us." The fire flickered in front of Yasunobu's face and Chiko felt Akifumi slide his hand into his. "It is a creature of power and beauty, and we must make it happy as we live in its home. We must treat this spirit with love and respect, for when we make it angry it roars with giant earthquakes and storms. We must look after it, and in turn it will protect us."

Chiko squeezed Akifumi's hand and vowed never to upset the *Tokai-Kaibutsu* again.

Three long months passed in Chiko's home under the city and in time memory of his former existence became submerged like a dream. A week after he'd first arrived he'd found the *thin* place and with that his position among the street boys had been secured. It was on the day of Chiko's seventh visit to the *thin* place that he was snatched away from this life, too.

It is safe to say that before that day Chiko was actually content - he had become well established among Tokyo's street children in the ruined, forgotten underbelly of the city. The children took it in turns to go 'foraging' to the surface for food at night and they were rarely caught. The group stuck together and all slept like curled up puppies in a forgotten hollow below one of the underground now-disused subway tracks. The quake and the explosions it had caused necessitated lots of rebuilding and often the city planners decided it was cheaper to start things afresh rather than repair the existing damaged structure. There were many children killed that day in February and perhaps many more like Chiko, who after becoming lost in the dust and sirens had found refuge underground with the existing homeless children. In this bewildering underground maze it never occurred to him to go to the surface for help; the little boy simply got on with where he found himself.

Although Chiko made his home with eleven other kids his best friends became three other boys: Akifumi, Yasunobu and Taisuke. The four boys played lots of games together and took turns to keep watch for each other when stealing on the surface. Chiko was especially popular with his friends because he was the one who had first discovered the *thin* place. The *thin* place was the most closely guarded secret the four of them had ever known; not even the rest of their gang knew about it. The *thin* place was something so special they rarely spoke of it aloud but instead alluded to it with a facial expression or hand gesture. Chiko was never entirely sure how he'd found it in the first place; it felt as though he'd sensed its existence in the air like the taint of blood in an empty room. He'd sniffed it out - followed it like a homing pigeon - and eventually had come upon it with a sense of satisfaction. He ignored the bad feelings the place produced and tried to concentrate on the wonder it provoked in his friends. It was difficult to get to and on the 24th April he took them to it for what would be the last time.

Spring was starting sluggishly that year - the weather was still cold and it rained often. The four boys ignored the dismal weather – they were happy because they'd stolen enough food this morning to last them for a few days and now they were going to the *thin* place. The city rose up all around them, jagged concrete teeth and grimy towers rearing high into the grey skies. Clouds the colour of purple bruises swarmed and chased one another, the mottled collection allowing no chink of sunlight. The four boys hadn't seen sunlight for weeks, but they had found something better than sunlight to play in.

"Hurry up!" Akifumi hissed at Chiko, pulling on his coat-sleeve to hurry his pace. Chiko was the smallest of their rag-tag group and if not for the fact they always waited for him he would be falling behind.

"We can go slower." Yasunobu flashed a stern glance at Akifumi even as he stretched his long legs to overtake. Taisuke kept his silence, his eyes not even following the exchange.

The boys continued to run through the deserted alleyways, around the upturned garbage cans and underneath criss-crossing laundry lines. The grey concrete of the streets echoed the grey sky overhead. The stench of rotten meat and exhaust fumes hung heavy in the air, and somewhere far away came the grumblings of heavy traffic and shrill voices shouting. Yasunobu fancied that the closer they got to the *thin* place the farther away the sounds were. As they entered the disused warehouse the city noises near disappeared, muted by the *thin* place. The four boys slowed to a silent walk. Chiko trailed his right hand along the bare walls and Akifumi chewed his bottom lip. They didn't look at each other as they wound their way downwards through the dusty corridors and the dim open spaces. Eventually the stairs took them into the basement and from there Chiko led them through a crack in the plaster down into the building's foundations and then into a fissure in the earth that widened out into a cave when they got deep enough. The boys hadn't figured out how to get here from the underground areas they usually spent their time in – the only way they knew was the one Chiko had discovered from the surface.

As they approached it their breathing sped up and Taisuke smiled faintly. They crawled around the last empty packing crates, and then they were there. The four boys approached the *thin* place in a cathedral like hush, wide eyed and reverent.

"Whoop!" Taisuke suddenly cried out and danced a little jig. The sound broke the tension and echoed through the space. Akifumi punched him on the arm. Taisuke grinned and sat on the floor. One by one the others followed, until only Chiko was left standing.

The youngest of the group remained on his feet, his eyes glazed. The boys were in a low, dark tunnel deep in the foundations of the city. Concrete blocks had bowed inwards on all sides and crumbled into tiny dusty pellets. The floor was bare except for the rubbish of bent metal and pieces of stone. They didn't know what this tunnel had once been used for.

Chiko wasn't staring at anything inside the space but rather at a faint ray of light that shone straight down though the tunnel as if from a hole in the roof. The narrow beam of light wasn't yellow enough to be called sunlight, and it was so insubstantial one could almost miss it, but the boys had seen it. It certainly didn't come from the surface above and there were no electronic lights around to have caused it. Chiko was staring at it - staring through it – so intently that he could have counted the glowing dust-motes that hung suspended within it. The little boy breathed softly and he could see the dust dancing to his breath all around the ray of light, but inside the beam the dust hung still.

Chiko turned around to his friends and with a flourish drew a spoon from his pocket. Very, very gently, Chiko turned back to the ray of light and passed the spoon through it. He shut his eyes and dropped the spoon from his fingers. There was a moment of silence and then the three boys behind him murmured and laughed. Chiko smiled and opened his eyes.

The spoon hung next to the dust-motes in the empty air.

CHAPTER 5

The mind drifted in its emerald seas, watching the dim underwater lights shift in their ever-changing configurations of spirals and stars. It saw everything through a faint green veil – the lights lay deep under the waves and it took great effort to watch them. They were so little and moved so fast. When it did manage to focus on its charge it rumbled and half-flipped with rage and fear. Men were chasing her.

The seas boiled with anger as the creature moved closer through the shadows, propelling itself through the green depths towards its sunken city.

* * *

Blaine chased the men through the winding alleyways of the city and cursed his luck. He'd finally found the girl only to discover she already had two other gunmen on her tail. Somewhere far ahead Bunny's heels clattered in the darkness and a drop of rain splashed onto Blaine's hair. He could hardly see a thing – the night sky was completely black and there seemed to be no streetlamps in this part of the city. After the next rumble of thunder the gunmen in front made their move. Blaine saw them crouch down far in the distance and that was all the warning he need to flatten himself into another wall.

Two shots rang out – *crack, crack* – and Blaine stiffened. He suddenly became very aware of the clammy bricks against his buttocks, the muggy stillness of the air and the silence into which you could hear a pin drop. His pulse was racing and there was a bitter taste in his mouth. The silence stretched into one, two, three heartbeats. It seemed to Blaine that the very city was holding its breath.

Tracking Bunny to the night club had been a difficult process but a short one. After checking into his hotel early the evening before Blaine had slept for an hour and then had awoken jet-lagged and hungry. He decided to start his search for Bunny the next morning. In the meantime, he needed food and exercise if he wanted to sleep through the night and adjust himself to Japanese time.

Blaine pulled himself up off the bed and put on some jeans and a blue t-shirt. He splashed his face with water, took his wallet and locked his bedroom door before leaving. As he took the elevator down the innards of the building he looked at his reflection. Running his hand over face he realised that he still hadn't shaved and his stubble was getting so long it could soon pass for a beard. There were dark bags under his eyes and his black hair was tousled from sleep. Blaine gave himself an ironic grin and ran a hand through his hair. He hummed softly as he made his way out of the hotel onto the street… and then halted in amazement. The place was heaving! When the taxi had dropped Blaine off he'd thought this street was relatively quiet, containing mainly shops and restaurants. Now though the street had come alive and Blaine realised he'd managed to pick a hotel right outside the night markets.

It was nearly 9:30pm but the air was still warm and humid. Streetlamps lit up the sky and there was no hope of seeing a horizon because the view was obscured in all directions by towering buildings that rose over sixty feet in the air. Windows winked back the reflections of huge electronic billboards, hanging lanterns and obscenely pink neon signs. The streets were packed with people and food stalls that sold noodles, fruit and skewered meat. The commotion filled the road and only one lane was left open to traffic. That traffic mainly consisted not of cars but of people on bicycles or motorbikes with strange little two-seater canopies on the back. Everyone seemed to be smoking or talking, the noise level was horrendous. Pop music blared out from a variety of shops, stall-keepers called out to each other and motor horns roared in the background. As Blaine moved slowly down the street people grabbed at him from all sides – stallholders touting their wares, small children wanting to touch the white man's clothes, a woman that ran her hand shyly down his back then turned away. Blaine kept one hand lightly over the pocket of his jeans holding his wallet. After the noise and the heat the smells struck him next. Frying meat, roasting nuts, a slight under-tang of garbage and sweat. Blaine's nose had a mind of its own, urging its owner closer towards the food stalls. Blaine strolled over to a stall that consisted of a metal counter that somehow doubled as a cooker. A woman sat on a high stool behind it.

When she saw Blaine she gave a toothless grin and cackled. *"Nihonryoori?"*

Blaine nodded and smiled, looking at the contents of the metal containers. There seemed to be plain noodles, some sort of cooked meat, noodles in soup and a pot of brown sludgy liquid he couldn't identify. Blaine pointed towards the soup noodles and the woman scooped some up into a paper carton.

"Mizu?" She asked, pointing to the bottles of water set into an ice bucket beside her.

"Yes thanks," Blaine replied with an encouraging nod.

The lady held up ten fingers – ¥1000 – and Blaine counted it out into her open palm before tucking the water under one arm and walking off with the noodles.

"Chotto matte!" The lady called, waving a pair of chopsticks.

"Thanks," Blaine said with another smile, moving backwards to take them. The woman grinned again, showing her gums and black teeth.

Blaine started off again, tucking the bottle into the back pocket of his jeans and picking up the noodles adeptly with the chopsticks. The food was greeted with a growl from his stomach and it tasted wonderful. It was spicy and although slightly oily it was very tasty. Blaine chewed thoughtfully as he walked deeper into the stalls. He passed acres of handbag and clothing stalls, ones containing painted plates and ornamental chopsticks, three whole stalls containing wallets and one with garden ornaments. As he moved deeper into the market the streetlamps petered out until he could hardly see the edges of the buildings on either side of the street. What light there was came from the electric lamps and candles lit around the stalls. He passed whole rows of tapes, videos and DVDs – a teenager with spiky blue hair stared at him until he was out of eyeshot – and saw women standing in doorways wearing very few clothes. The last shadowy section of stalls was a group of tables on which rested mobile phones, machine parts and electronic devices.

Blaine suddenly realised that this might be the place to buy a gun. He had intended to go to a shop tomorrow but wouldn't this be better? This way he could not be tracked later by the authorities. He moved closer to the stall containing the machine parts and, sure enough, tucked underneath one of the tables were some empty gun holsters. A young Japanese man approached him and spoke in halting English.

"What you look for?"

Blaine shrugged and pointed to the holsters. "These?"

"We only sell these. No guns."

"Ah, okay." Blaine said quietly, aware that the youth was summing him up.

"You want guns?" he whispered.

Blaine nodded.

"Okay." The man motioned him towards the doorway of a building beside the stall. "Here."

Blaine followed the man and together they stepped into one of the grimy buildings and took the third door on the left into a small, dark room.

"Here," said the youth with a grin.

He pulled out a drawer from a large clothing chest and revealed a miniature stock pile of arms. Blaine blinked in amazement – he had not for a moment imagined it would be so easy. He touched one of the revolvers.

"How much?"

And so they set to haggling. Blaine eventually walked away with the gun having paid nearly two hundred pounds, which was more than he'd have paid buying it legitimately in England but well worth the price considering it was a black market weapon and hopefully untraceable to him.

When he and the youth exited the building twenty-five minutes later they were both smiling and Blaine wondered where to go next. He considered going deeper into the shadowy alleyways of the city but after quick consideration dismissed the idea. He waved to the youth as he turned right and began to walk away, throwing his noodles carton into a bin shaped like a dragon and heading towards his hotel.

Blaine had awoken at 8:00am the morning after arriving in Tokyo, feeling fresh and surprisingly well-adjusted to his new time zone. He took a shower and when he got dressed took care to pack his new gun and the documents he would need for the day ahead. He made his way downstairs – no sign of the receptionist again – and stepped outside of the hotel blinking in the grey daylight. It was hot and humid with dark clouds threatening on the horizon.

The streets were busy but still far quieter than they had been the night before; a few vendors were selling noodles and water but there were none of the huge stalls of yesterday. Blaine studied the now-open shops that lined the streets and wandered into one that looked like a bakery. Inside he pointed at some pastries and a water bottle and was gratified when the purchase went seamlessly. He munched on the pastry – a small croissant-like thing filled with sausage – and debated how best to get a taxi. He had already decided that he would not risk getting lost by using the subway

- his guidebook contained a subway map and the multi-coloured, myriad maze of routes looked like a recipe for never finding his bearings again.

After small consideration he walked over to a line of motorcycles that had the strange canopies attached to the back. He showed them the address that KT had got for him, the address where Bunny's laptop was last registered as being used at. The first driver shook his head and folded his arms but the second nodded eagerly, pushing Blaine into the narrow seat behind the motorbike saddle. He sat down on the hard seat and with a roar the engine sprang to life. As the bike darted forwards Blaine hung on tightly, the driver riding at high speed through the busy streets. He wound fearlessly around cars, fruit vendors and pedestrians. The drive took over twenty minutes and as it proceeded Blaine realised he was being taken into the poorer parts of the city. The buildings began to get grubbier and there were no more decorative slanting roofs or drainpipes. The people wandering around didn't wear suits and the dozens of children playing at each corner wore ripped clothes and looked unwashed. Suddenly they came out into a relatively open space and the driver pointed his arm, crying: *"Jishin!"*

Blaine followed his finger and realised that the open space was not put there by design. This was where the Valentine's Day Earthquake had occurred. Blaine had been given to understand that the rebuilding had started over the destruction zone but there was no such activity going on here.

The demolished area was about half a mile square and in the space where more buildings would have stood lay only mounds and mounds of broken concrete, spaghetti strands of twisted steel and smashed glass. The glass glinted like jewels amongst the rubble and dust. The driver made clucking sounds and motioned for Blaine to get off the bike. Confused, he did so and stood facing the wreckage. This was the first place in the city he'd seen anything approaching a horizon but only because the immediate buildings had been floored to make way for it. Blaine stood gazing at the destruction with his hands in his pockets, like a gunslinger overlooking a desert. He wondered what happened in the spaces the quake had created underground, whether or not the subways were being repaired. Blaine's driver tugged on his sleeve and made clicking noises again. Blaine frowned at him and held his hands out wide to indicate his confusion. The driver began hopping slightly and this time in addition to the clicking noise he waggled his forefinger in front of his face and screwed one eye shut. Blaine stared at him in incomprehension until realisation dawned.

"No, no," he said angrily, mindless of the fact the driver didn't speak English. "I'm not going to take photos of this. No. Carry on driving, please."

The man ducked his head and got back onto the seat of his motorbike, driving his ungrateful passenger to his original destination.

When they arrived at yet another nondescript street and the man pointed to a grey building indistinguishable from the rest Blaine realised two things. One, it was probably not a good idea to offend a taxi driver in a foreign country when you had no idea where you were going. Two, he was going to be horribly over-charged for this little excursion. With a sigh he handed over the Yen and stood on the pavement looking up at the buildings while the motorbike roared off.

Blaine compared the Japanese characters on the slip of paper in his wallet to those written on the frontages of the buildings and entered the door below the ones that matched. He wandered through the open archway and found himself immediately faced with a wide set of stairs that were wooden and painted black. The walls were also black and adorned with *anime* posters. When he reached the top Blaine saw why. This place was an internet café, or a games workshop of some kind. Dozens of computers sat in neat rows and Japanese boys were dotted amongst them, some sitting in small groups and some alone. All of the teenagers wore leather and had facial piercings or dyed hair. Blaine walked over to a group of half a dozen kids crowded around two computers in one corner. They were chattering excitedly and occasionally pointing at the screens. Blaine tried to see what they were looking at but most of the screens were filled with writing.

"Hi," he said with a wave and a smile. "Do any of you speak English?"

As one the boys turned around to stare at him. Blaine fixed the smile on his face, hoping that at least one of them might speak his language. None of them replied. Blaine waited a few moments more then unfolded the picture of Bunny from his pocket. "I'm looking for my cousin, this lady here. She's gone missing and her laptop was registered as being used at this address. I hoped that maybe one of you would have seen her?"

A few of the boys looked at each other but they all stayed silent. Blaine made a show of looking at the photograph again. "I really need to find her."

One of the boys tilted his chin up. He wore a black t-shirt with neon purple characters across the chest and his hair was spiked vertically upwards from his forehead.

"She your cousin?" He spoke curtly and Blaine couldn't tell if it was the result of his demeanour or his accent.

"Yeah. She's gone missing, she had an argument with her father but now I really need to find her."

"We steal no laptop." The boy's eyes glittered.

"No, of course not." Blaine held out his hands. "I just thought that maybe she used it here, or sold it to you."

The group visibly relaxed. "Yeah, maybe." The boy stretched out his hand and Blaine gave him the picture. *"Kirei na onna no ko,"* he said to his mates and they laughed leeringly. Blaine tried not to let his irritation show. "She come here, maybe two month ago. She say she need to sell. Our friend buy. ¥70,000." He shrugged. "Don't know where she go though."

Blaine's heart began to beat faster – his wild goose chase was paying off. "Is your friend here? Do you know where she went - if she's still in the city?"

"No." The boy turned his back on Blaine and the whole group refocused on their game.

Their backs literally turned, Blaine sighed. Another clue on the goose chase would have been helpful. He retraced his steps back out through the computer banks and down the stairs. Just before he got to the bottom he heard a noise. Turning his head to the left Blaine saw one of the younger boys – perhaps ten years old – hissing at him from a recessed alcove in the side of the stairwell.

"Mister," the boy called. He wore a hugely oversized American baseball cap. "How much you pay for woman?"

"Some," said Blaine cautiously. "You know where she is?"

"I take you to her. Tonight. ¥11,000."

Blaine laughed. "¥2,000."

"You never find her without me. No Japanese."

"¥5,000 then."

"¥5,000." The boy's grubby face creased into a smile. "Okay-ey, ¥5,000. Meet me tonight, 11:00pm, outside Fumi Kurabu Disuko."

Blaine shook his head. "I don't know where that is."

"Here." The boy produced a slip of paper and scrawled some characters across it. "You show taxi, meet 11:00pm. Okay-ey?"

Blaine smiled, bemused. "Okay-ey."

Eleven hours later Blaine found himself standing outside a brightly lit nightclub, the slip of paper tightly clutched in one hand. He'd caught a taxi from the bottom of his street where the traffic was still flowing to avoid the congestion caused by the night market. He'd showed the piece of paper to the driver and the man had leered at him but waved him into the backseat. It was a proper taxi this time: a car and not a motorbike. Blaine settles into the leather seat that smelled of pine air freshener and cigarettes and watched the lights of the city go past. The drive took about twenty-five minutes - Blaine kept having to remind himself how big this city was. Eventually the car began to slow down on a street that was crowded with brightly lit bars, takeaway stalls and nightclubs. Neon lights flashed from every wall and doorway, the odd billboard glittered its plastic adverts out of the darkness. They pulled up outside a nightclub with flashing blue windows and high tables with people drinking behind them.

"This is it?" Blaine pointed from the piece of paper to the club.

"*Koko.*"

"Okay, thanks." Blaine paid the man and got out.

He'd already forgotten that he was speaking to people even though they didn't understand his language – it just felt good to be speaking aloud. Blaine stood on the pavement and looked up at the building. Two large security guards stood outside and the odd person wandered in up the steps between them to get inside. Dance music was pumping out through the open glass doors and the girls visible through the opening wore brightly coloured, skimpy clothes. The place looked grand and expensive. Blaine started up the stone steps himself but was stopped by a familiar-sounding hiss. Blaine peered round the side of the steps and saw the boy from the gaming place crouched down behind them. He wondered why he was hiding – perhaps the doormen would send off an underage boy if they caught him loitering.

The boy gestured with one hand to show that Blaine should follow him. Gaining a few funny looks from the bouncers, Blaine turned around on the steps and moved down onto the street. The boy kept crouched down, moving in the gutter in the shadows of parked cars. He took Blaine right down to the end of the street – next to what looked like a huge strip joint – before making a sudden left into an alley. The alley was perhaps three feet wide and Blaine touched the gun holster underneath his shirt. Once they were safely ensconced in the shadows the boy whispered something Blaine couldn't hear.

"I'm sorry?"

"She no there. She in *hen kurabu disuko*."

"What does that mean?"

The boy merely shrugged and continued on. He led Blaine through a maze of tiny, narrow alleys with broken paving stones and disposable chopsticks lying in gutters. The buildings rose high on all sides and towered over the two of them, their tops shrouded in darkness. The alleys were completely dark except for the odd streetlamps that flickered from behind corners; the shadows were deep and black and everything from broken chairs to the edges of buildings to the boy's silhouette was tinged with green. Blaine could smell sewers and rubbish but strangely there was no noise. The constant hum of the city emanating from traffic and blaring music was gone; in its place was a cathedral hush broken only by the footfalls of Blaine and his guide. Blaine shivered in the clammy air; this midnight walk was eerie. He looked up when thunder rumbled far away. The city with its strange shadowy quietness and ominous weather was getting to him.

"This place gives me the creeps."

The boy shot him a queer sidelong look. "The *Tokai-Kaibutsu* is angry tonight. We go quickly."

"The what?"

The boy put a finger over his lips. "You foreigner." In silence he continued to lead Blaine into the night.

After a timeless while the boy led Blaine out of one deserted alleyway into another that backed out onto a narrow street with a concrete warehouse at the far end. Music was booming out of the place but no bouncers stood outside on the dimly lit steps; this place looked grimy and unfriendly.

"There," the boy pointed. Then he held out his hand for money.

Blaine looked at him disbelievingly but paid anyway. He had followed him this far, after all. As soon as the money touched his palm the boy slid away into the darkness, becoming another grey shadow in a city of shadows.

Blaine touched his gun holster again and started towards the nightclub. Above him there came a low rumble of thunder but no rain yet. Blaine was sweating in his shirt, he didn't think it would be long before the storm broke. He entered the doorway hesitantly and as soon as he did a tall, heavyset man stepped in front of him. The bouncer wordlessly looked Blaine up and down, his eyes giving away nothing, then nodded for Blaine to step through. A woman beside him sitting at a desk held up two fingers: ¥2,000. Blaine paid silently, when the volume of the music was so high the language barrier fell out of existence. The woman motioned him down some steep stairs from where the hard bass and blinking lights were emanating. Blaine stepped down them carefully and eventually found himself in a dark, low-ceilinged basement with a make-shift bar at one end and a dance floor at the other. Blaine bought himself a drink by the simple expedient of pointing and then took a walk around the club. It was full of Japanese youngsters with dyed streaks in their hair and beer in their hands – although many of them were so spaced out and wide eyed Blaine doubted they were just ingesting alcohol. He circled the club, saw a couple kissing up against a wall and a pair of boys swallowing capsules that looked like hard mints. Everyone was in their twenties and wore lots of tight-fitting, black leather. The room was lit with green floor lights that provided an ominous contrast to the flashing multi-coloured strobe lights. The green darkness of this hole echoed the city above it in some way that made Blaine feel uncomfortable. As he walked around he studied the patrons, looking for Bunny. The dim lighting made it hard for him to see anyone clearly and he relied mainly on impressions: the sharp curve of a young girl's cheek too rounded to be Bunny's, a man's long dark hair, a short woman with pitch-black eyes. Blaine was starting to despair of finding his mark… until he did.

He rounded a curve of the bar until he was staring out into the centre of the dance floor… and there she was. Her blond hair stood out like a beacon underneath the strobes and her face was upturned into the light as if she were worshipping a god. Blue shadows flitted over her cheekbones and there was a smudge of ultra-violet paint on her collarbone. Her eyes were closed but her mouth was slightly open as she danced to the grungy music with its hard bass with her hands and her hips and her feet. Her hands were entrancing; the fingers moved sinuously through the air as if they were trying to stroke and cup the sound with the shapes they made in the darkness. All around her glowsticks burnt pink trails into the darkness.

Blaine seated himself on a bench set into the curved alcove in front of the bar and stared at the object of his search with his mouth open. Beside him a young couple were practically copulating on the seat but he ignored them. Blaine gripped his drink tightly and just stared at Bunny. This was the girl he'd chased halfway around the world to find, who'd successfully murdered her father and escaped a nationwide police hunt. This was her… flying high and dancing the night away in an underground Japanese nightclub. He studied her intently, feeling a mix of satisfaction at having found her and anger that it had taken so much effort to find such a drugged-up idiot. In the darkness she and the other dancers looked like grim puppets arching to the bass, parasites on the music. In the right light the dancers looked like fish - all slim and sinewy sliding underwater. Blaine shook his head in amazement and continued to watch Bunny for nearly an hour, barely sipping at his beer.

As Blaine sat there, a casual observer on the sidelines, he became part of the furniture and perhaps that was why he wasn't seen as a threat by the two Japanese men also watching her from the other side of the dance floor. Blaine noticed them when Bunny peeled away from the other dancers and headed towards the bar. She passed just a few feet away from him and it gave him a strange thrill to see her in her tight black dress and metallic heels. Her blond hair was mussed and her eyes were smudged with kohl, all dark and wide. She had a light, graceful way of winding around the low tables and entwined couples. Several men trailed her with their eyes but the only one who got up to follow her was a middle-aged, short man in a suit. He looked very out of place and as Blaine studied him he also noticed the bulge underneath one of the arms of his suit jacket.

Blaine watched carefully as the suit-man followed Bunny to the bar then, after she bought a bottle of water, followed her back to the dance floor. Once she was dancing again the suit-man rejoined his friend and the two of them settled down at a table to watch her. Blaine frowned to himself and tried to appear as unobtrusive as possible. That was, admittedly, difficult considering he was a tall white man in a Japanese nightclub. Nonetheless he stayed still and remained unnoticed for another two hours, when at 3:00am Bunny decided she'd had enough for the night. It was obvious where she was headed when she made neither for the bar nor the ladies' toilets but for the cloakroom.

Blaine followed her at some distance from the suit-men, who remained no more than ten feet away from her at all times. Blaine was amazed she didn't notice them but perhaps she was too far gone into the pretty strobes lights. She certainly seemed high - she smiled vacantly at the cloakroom attendant and then drowsily slipped on a short leather jacket. Her dress was cut short and poofed out slightly on the skirt part, the jacket only zipped down to her hips. On a fatter woman that might have emphasised unsightly curves but on Bunny it only served to show how reduced to skin and bones she was. Blaine's eyes studied her slim calves as she climbed up the stairs to the exit. The spike of one of her stilettos glinted in the darkness. The two suit-men followed quickly after her and Blaine followed behind them.

And that was how Blaine came to be following the three of them through the dark city. Once they were outside the club Blaine remained some distance from the three in front, dropping back so that he kept only the two men in sight. Outside the air was even hotter than it had been in the sweaty basement and Blaine could feel static crackling in the atmosphere. The men set off into one of the tiny, crazed alleys and Blaine followed behind. The odd raindrop splashed down but whenever he looked up no more followed. Thunder kept rumbling and Blaine pressed himself behind some metal steps fixed to a brick wall as the men looked around. That eerie hush fell again as they turned left, then right and then left again down the dark green alleys. Blaine wondered where the girl was headed, where she thought she was leading these three men into the night.

When the shots rang out – *crack, crack* - Blaine pressed himself even flatter against the wall and waited desperately to hear more. Had they killed her?

He counted his heartbeats, hardly daring to breathe. And then there was sound. A fast, uneven clicking punctuated the night followed by heavier, more rhythmic thuds. Blaine realised he was listening to the sound of Bunny's heels as she sprinted away and the gunmen followed her. Blaine burst into action: this is what he'd been trained for. Just because he didn't understand what was unfolding didn't mean he wanted to miss it. His sneakers pounded down on the uneven surfaces as he ran, jumping over garbage cans and winding around piles of rubbish and discarded furniture. The alleys were still dark and he still couldn't see the tops of the buildings. There seemed not to be another soul in the world - just the four of them locked in this endless chase. Suddenly there was a yelp from the men up ahead and one of them fell to the ground, clutching his leg.

The night got blacker and a second drop of rain fell on Blaine's cheek. This time when he looked up the heavens opened. Rain pattered down and lightening flashed overhead. The water fell softly at first and then harder until it was pounding down onto concrete, brick, panes of glass and the running figures below. What little light filtered into the alley from adjoining ones began to reflect oddly off the wet surfaces. Black windowpanes began to reflect blue sheens, pipes and gutters glistened and the walls of the buildings ran with green rain. It was as if the world had become monochrome; only blacks and greens were allowed. Under cover of the storm Blaine moved steadily forward to where the two men huddled on the ground. They had stopped just before a cross-junction and Blaine thought that Bunny had run across straight through it. He paused, just a few feet away in the thick sheets of hammering water, and tried to see why they'd halted. When he saw the scarlet blood flowing on to the ground he leaned closer and understood. The taller of the suit-men had fallen during the chase and impaled his leg on a piece of metal fallen loose from one of the many metal fire escapes that grew up the sides of the buildings. He must have tripped and fallen heavily on it because the metal had gone straight through his calf. Blaine doubted that the injury was life-threatening but it was obvious the man wouldn't be doing any more running tonight. As he leaned over to watch them he suddenly saw movement from the corner of his right eye. He looked up and saw a small pale face staring straight at him from the alley on the right-hand turn of the crossroad. She must have looped back to see what had happened to her 'two' pursuers. Blaine felt for his gun but in a flash of blond hair she was off. He sprinted after her like a dog chasing a rabbit, mindless of the two men left behind crouching in the rain.

They yelled out angrily: *"Yame, yamete!"*

Distantly Blaine heard three more shots ring out behind him but he was already too far gone, chasing this pale shape that flitted through the black city before him. She darted in and out of passageways and doorways, her blond hair once illuminated orange by a dying streetlamp. Blaine chased her hard, his clothes soaked with rain and his feet slipping on wet stones. His gun was clutched in his right hand and his blue eyes were wild as he pushed himself to keep up with her but she suddenly blinked out of sight, like a wraith.

Blaine stood stock still in yet another deserted alleyway, listening for her over the rain and his beating heart. His gun was cocked, the barrel pointing upwards into the sky. There was a dead-end to his left and the alley continued on into darkness up ahead but he thought she'd stopped somewhere along here. A neon pink sign fizzled in Japanese high on the building to his right, one character was dim and another flickered on and off. The pink refracted strangely off the rain and caused a puddle below to shine red. He was totally still, his head tilted to one side as he listened. His hair was plastered to his skull with water. *There!* A nearby crunch, made by someone who wanted to be quiet. He swung his head around like a wolf and was gratified to see movement in the shadows of the dead-end as the prey turned to flee. Blaine jumped after her but more slowly this time; he knew the alley was blocked because he could see a building rising up at the end of it. She had nowhere left to run. He advanced slowly, his pupils widening as he grew accustomed to the even dimmer light.

The shadows in this pathway between the high-rise buildings seemed darker than ever, their edges tinged with an even stronger shade of green. Blaine jogged forwards, willing his eyes to adjust, and then saw a thing that he would carry with him in dreams for the rest of his life.

Bunny was backed-up, half curled against the cracking concrete wall. She'd lost a stiletto somewhere along the way and now held the other tightly in her right hand. Her bare legs were white and mud-splashed, her clothes were soaked and stuck to her skin. Her blond hair was curled across her shoulders and forehead, her mouth was open in an 'o' of surprise.

Her eyes were what captivated Blaine – were what stalled him for that crucial second and prevented him from firing the gun. Her eyes swam in the pale lines of her face, dark ovals with glints of green in the centre. Her mascara had run down her cheeks and was smeared all over her eyelids but that only seemed to accentuate those wide orbs more. Blaine blinked away his stupefaction and raised his gun and fired... but it was already too late. Bunny turned her body away and then *melted* into the wall like a shadow before the bullet reached her.

Blaine continued to stand there, firing bullet after bullet and then blank after blank, into the wet glistening concrete for an hour after.

CHAPTER 6

The mind drifted in its green depths, pulled by strong tides and remorseless currents. The lights of the city were submerged, sunk beneath the dark waters, pinpoints of lanterns lost beneath the waves. Everything was dark and the air was thick and humid, too hot for anything other than more sheets of warm rain. It was night time here, it was always night time when it awoke. Tonight, like last night, the starry furniture of the heavens was obscured by thick black clouds. The mind stretched, its dumb consciousness as slow and primal as an ancient jellyfish. Tendrils of awareness stirred in the night and it found the wound again, worried at it, tasted it. A slow shuddering then started somewhere deep in its innards and the creature paused, hanging still in its liquid firmament.

Worried, it sought the girl, and found her sleeping in a warm ball in her makeshift bed of ill-fitting sheets and clothes. Her room was very small, in addition to the single bed it contained a stove and a desk but not much else. She was dreaming, thinking she was protected here in the centre of the beast. A computer winked in the corner, its screensaver a roiling mass of green trees that moved ceaselessly. On the stove sat a small saucepan, dirtied with traces of green soup. Mascara was still smudged over her eyes and her petite, naked right foot twitched where it lay outside of the covers. A roll of small bills and casino chips were scattered on the desk, next to a screw of paper containing crumbling white pills. The room was dark except for the blinking computer screen; it had no windows and smelt of food. Beside the bed, next to three empty coffee mugs, lay a passport and a knife. In the bathroom painkillers were stashed next to tubes of eyeliner and lipstick. The bed-sit was dark and cramped, like a cave. The girl was very alone.

With great care, the mind extended another tendril of green consciousness towards her, designed to awaken and to warn…

* * *

After the incident with the wall Blaine sat on the bed in his tiny hotel room, huddled like a child in blankets. He watched the rain fall down onto the street below. It was 5:00am and still pitch black outside, the rain and the lightening still warring. He was a grown man and he had just seen an impossible thing.

He stared fixedly out of the glass, watching the rain splash down on it and hearing its steady drumming on the roof as if he could wish what had happened earlier that night away. He wanted to believe it was a hallucination, that somehow his drink in the club had been spiked or that it was all a bad dream, but he couldn't force himself to believe either of these things. No more than he thought the flying pumpkins had been thrown by trick-or-treaters. He was wearing a pair of boxer shorts and a thick woollen jumper, his wet clothes lay discarded at the foot of the bed. He knew he needed a shower to warm up but somehow couldn't force himself to stand under more running water. So instead he was wrapped up in a spare blanket he'd found underneath the bed and was half-covered by the duvet too. Nothing had shaken him this badly since – *since he'd killed... no, don't think of Lilly* – since he'd left the police. The most likely explanation for the evening's events was that Blaine was going insane. Going? Gone. But he didn't feel insane. Was there a way insanity felt? Did you know when you were going mad? *Perhaps the first clue is when you see girls disappearing into walls.* Blaine shook his head and tried to focus on the raindrops running down his windowpane. They were silvery-blue and left snaking trails down the dark glass. Eventually he slept.

Blaine awoke five hours later feeling better that the night has passed but no less dislocated from the world. He was in a country where no one spoke his language, he hadn't had a proper meal in days and he'd just seen a girl vanish into a wall. He was feeling afloat, a drifting spar of flotsam in a deep ocean. It took some effort to resist clutching at the sides of the mattress to check it was still there and concrete. He'd come so close to completing the job he was hired for he could taste it... could still see himself aiming his gun at the girl's head and pulling the trigger. And who the hell were the two suit-men? He had an inkling but ignored it for now. First things first. He pulled himself out of bed – he was still fully clothed – and felt with distaste how clammy his skin was. He shucked off the boxers and jumper and hopped into the tiny shower. He put the water onto its hottest setting and lay his head back against the tiles to luxuriate in it. Blaine shut his eyes and let the hot water pound heat into his bones. After a few minutes he scrubbed shampoo into his hair and then rinsed it out. Once he felt scrubbed fresh and was getting hot he switched the shower off, wrapped himself in the fluffy towel and had a shave. When he'd finished in the bathroom he came out and picked his wet clothes up from last night… and got a nasty surprise.

Hidden inside his soggy jeans was a satin black stiletto with a snapped metal heel. Blaine picked the shoe up and sat down on the bed, turning it over and over in his hands. He felt like a cross between a Prince and a relic hunter, holding Cinderella's mythical shoe. He'd picked it up in an alley near the nightclub whilst retracing his steps to get a taxi home last night. It had seemed like such a lost, precious thing, an object born of night and shadow. He'd carried it the whole way back here, the heel pressed tightly into his palm. Blaine sighed and placed the shoe reverently on the bed. At least he knew he had not hallucinated that part of the midnight chase. He hung his wet clothes up to dry on the narrow radiator and pulled on his only other pair of jeans and another t-shirt. Then he rifled through his guidebook and set off into the streets of Tokyo.

Once outside the hotel he wandered over to the line of motorbike taxis and hailed one. This time the first driver he asked agreed to go where Blaine wanted. The weather was tepid and dreary today, the storm having spent itself out. Grey clouds hung in a milky sky. Occasionally on the fifteen minute journey it rained a little but never for long. This time when they arrived Blaine recognised his destination. The Hilton reared up ahead of them, its English logo emblazoned proudly on the pink brick. It looked out of place among the Japanese-styled high-rises and seemed desperately American. Blaine almost smiled. Once the bike stopped outside the lobby Blaine paid the driver and gave him a small tip. He got out of the bizarre curtained seat and entered the light, air-conditioned lobby.

"Good afternoon sir," said the doorman with an American accent.

"Hi," Blaine replied with a grin. He liked Americans.

He wandered through the brightly decorated lobby, amazed at the facilities they had there for the Westerner away from home: clothes boutiques, a pharmacy, a photographic shop, an English-speaking movie theatre, two swimming pools, a gym and four blessed English-speaking restaurants. Of the latter there was the choice of McDonalds, Japanese, an Italian and a 'Ye Olde Irish Pub'. Blaine chuckled to himself at the last one but chose the Italian instead. He walked into the cold, air-conditioned restaurant and was gratified to find that even though it was lunchtime it was nearly empty.

"Just a table for one, sir?" A Japanese waiter with impeccable English approached him with a white dishcloth over one arm.

"Yes, please," Blaine said and was led to a small table in the corner with a red tablecloth and a rose in a small vase.

"What can I get you to drink?" The waiter asked as he handed Blaine a menu.

"Just some water, thanks."

"Very well." The waiter hurried off.

Blaine studied the menu and when the waiter returned he ordered fried brie to start, followed by meatballs with spaghetti in a tomato and thyme sauce. After placing his order Blaine sat back in his comfy chair and had a good think. What was he going to do next? One, he could continue as originally agreed: find Bunny Eury and try to kill her. Two, he could take Faber's advance and run. The second option would mean he could leave this mad place, leave Japan, leave Cinderella's shoe behind in his tiny hotel room. He didn't think he'd feel like he was breaking his contract; Faber had broken it anyway when he'd hired two other gunmen who'd tried to shoot Blaine as well as Bunny. And yet... Blaine's instincts were strangely set against taking the second option.

As his starter arrived – a great slab of brie on a bed of rocket and cherry tomatoes – he tried to work out why. Blaine was not a man accustomed to introspection but last night had disturbed him in ways he felt obliged to understand. There were a whole mixture of emotions roiling inside him: he'd been badly scared last night, he was angry because he'd been scared and he was desperate to know what had happened to that wall. He was experiencing the same sort of dread curiosity he'd felt watching horror movies as a young boy: you didn't want to watch the scary parts but something compelled you not to press the 'pause' button. Blaine nodded his thanks to the waiter as he efficiently cleared his plate away. And, he realised with another unsettling jolt, this was the first time he'd felt so strongly about anything since – *since her hair fanned out on the tiles* – since he'd left the police. It was unsettling and exciting. Blaine sipped his water and realised another thing about himself. He was many things, but he was not a coward. If he ran away now then that was somehow what he would have become... he felt like Alice before she went down the rabbit hole, like Neo being asked in *The Matrix* whether he wanted the red pill or the blue one.

A decision having been made in his subconscious, even if he hadn't vocalised it yet, Blaine slid his mobile out of his pocket and called Faber. He didn't bother to check what time it was in England; he suspected that Faber would take this call at any time of the day or night.

"Speak."

"Faber? It's Blaine."

"Ah. Have you found her yet?"

"Yeah. And I would've got her last night, too, if your other guys hadn't shown up."

There was silence. Blaine could hear Faber breathing. Five long seconds passed. "You saw them?"

"Yeah."

"So it was you."

"It was me what?"

"Who engineered that trap."

"What trap?"

Another pause. "You were there. You saw what happened?"

Blaine thought of the wall and his heart beat faster. "What do you mean?"

"You saw the trap that nearly took the leg off one of my 'other guys'."

"No, I didn't see that. I mean, I saw he got hurt… I just thought he tripped."

"No. Apparently a piece of metal was oddly balanced on the ground, the pipe came out from nowhere to pierce his leg. They insist it was rigged."

"Well, maybe. But not by me."

"But you were the one who chased after her? You didn't get her?"

"No. She… was too fast. She got away from me."

"I see." Faber's voice failed to disguise his contempt. "Do you anticipate success in the near future? I'm beginning to regret giving you that advance."

Blaine sighed, deliberately. He'd dealt with awkward clients before. "As I said, I *would* have got her if you hadn't gone behind my back hiring other people to do the same job. You didn't just screw up my work you endangered me in the process. They did tell you they shot at me, right? And you only know to hunt here at all because of *my* lead. I don't want them killing her first and nicking my fee."

"What is it you want?"

"For you to call them off. I'll do this quite happily on my own."

"No. I want as many people on her tail as I can."

"Then I want more money. Now. A little more on the advance - a finder's fee. To compensate me in case your other guys kill her before I do."

"That is not unreasonable. I will pay you another fifth of your total fee now. To receive the remaining three hundred thousand I expect her dead."

"That's fair. I'll let you know when it's done."

"Good." The line went dead.

Blaine snapped his phone shut just as the waiter brought over his pasta. He tucked into the steaming dish with a smile on his face – an extra hundred thousand guaranteed even if he didn't kill the girl could buy a lot of pasta.

After his gorgeous meal and successful negotiating session Blaine felt nearly human again. He wandered around the Hilton's lobby and bought a t-shirt and some more trainers because his had been fairly wrecked in the rain last night. He considered moving from his tiny hotel and staying here but in the end decided he was happy where he was. Whilst trying on some over-priced sunglasses he considered his next move. How was he to find this girl who didn't want to be found?

An hour later Blaine was standing outside the only place he could think of to answer that question: the internet café he'd visited before. He walked up the stairs feeling like an intruder again and as he stepped into the room full of computers he scanned it for the little boy that had led him so far last night. He spotted him crouching down with the same established group of boys he'd been with last time. Blaine doubted they ever went to school, they seemed to live here. The boy caught sight of Blaine and ducked down behind a table.

"Hey, hey." Blaine walked over to the group of boys, his tone friendly. "There's no problem, I just wanted to ask you for some more information."

The boy poked his delicate face up over the computer banks. "Just information?"

"Yeah." Blaine gestured with his right hand. "Wanna talk outside?"

"Okay-ey." The boy shot some looks to his friends but was clearly impressed at being pulled out of the crowd.

Once they were standing on the stairs again Blaine asked him what his name was.

"Kazuto." The boy replied.

"Kaz-ut-o." Blaine tried the name until he could pronounce it properly. When he finally succeeded the boy grinned.

"What you want?"

"The girl from last night, she got away. Do you know where she lives?"

"How much you pay?"

"¥4,000."

"¥12,000."

"¥8,000."

"Deal." The boy stuck out his pale brown paw and Blaine shook it. His fingers were tiny; they made Blaine revise his estimate of the kid's age downwards.

"Do you know where she lives?"

"No. But I find out."

"You're sure?" Blaine must have looked doubtful, because the boy looked affronted.

"Of course."

"Okay then. How long do you think it'll take?"

"Some hours. You have phone? I call you tonight."

Blaine scribbled his mobile number down on a scrap of paper. "Sometime tonight."

"Maybe tonight, maybe afternoon. See you later!" Kazuto darted back up the stairs.

Blaine walked down to his waiting taxi and wondered how he was going to kill the intervening time. He ended up going back to the Hilton, using the gym and the swimming pool and then watching a movie. Fittingly, they were showing *Constantine* – the story of a cynical, detached man searching a city beset with wraiths and demons. Blaine watched it impassively, munching stolidly on his popcorn. He'd never expected to identify with Keanu Reeves in any movie, let alone one filled with monsters from Heaven and Hell. He was aware his behaviour was slightly irrational, but he stubbornly avoided analysing it. The movie finished around 7:00pm and afterwards Blaine decided to sample another of the restaurants. He wasn't nearly as hungry as at lunch so this time he elected to try the Irish pub. He nearly laughed when he stepped inside – the place was brightly lit, clean and bedecked with green clover and leprechauns. The barman that greeted him was, quite improbably, wearing a green pixie cap.

"What can I get you, sir?"

"Just a beer, thanks." He sat down at the bar, smiling to himself. 'Ye Olde Irish Pub', indeed! He remembered the pubs his father had used to take him to: dark, smoky caverns filled with frosty old men.

Blaine sat back in the idealised bar and waited for his phone call. After a while he ordered a burger and after that he ordered another beer.

The call came at 9.30pm, just as Blaine was considering ordering dessert.

"Hello?" he said.

A familiar squeaky voice came back down the line. "Mister, I've found her but you must come quickly."

"She's on the move? I wanted you to find her flat."

"If you want her come to address." The phone clicked dead and ten seconds later Blaine received a picture message with two lines of Japanese characters on it. He figured that his phone wouldn't be configured right to receive a text message. He sighed and pulled himself out of the comfy booth. He nodded to the bar and left a tip on the table. Then he stepped outside, to find yet another taxi.

When the taxi dropped Blaine off it was nearing 11:00pm and this time there was no crowded street of nightclubs. Blaine realised as the taxi growled off that there were also no lights in this part of the city; once the car's headlights drew far enough away he was left in total blackness. The light of the crescent moon was just enough to make out the outlines of the tall buildings that crowded in on him but Blaine still felt claustrophobic and uneasy. He shifted from one foot to the other as he looked around the narrow street. The concrete buildings rearing up on either side were in a state of disrepair, with crumbling plaster and broken pieces of jagged glass in the windows. The windowpanes that were whole winked blackly into the night. Kazuto materialised out of the shadow of a nearby car.

"Come," he waved his little hand at Blaine and once again the bigger man followed.

Kazuto led Blaine into yet another alley that led off the street between two high-rise buildings; on his own Blaine doubted he would have spotted such a narrow passageway. Thunder rumbled somewhere far away and the air grew hot and full of static. Blaine tasted tin in the air. The alleyway was eighteen inches wide - Blaine kept having to duck under fire escapes and swerve around rubbish. He knew it was his imagination but he couldn't help feeling that the buildings with their impenetrable black windows were drawing slowly closer together as they walked. Green lights began to flicker in the corners of his vision but whenever he turned his head there was nothing there. He started to sweat a little and his eyes were dancing this way and that to hunt out the emerald flashes. The walls of the buildings took on a green hue as Kazuto led them down another of the mazelike passageways. The boy started to jog.

"Hurry," the boy breathed as thunder rumbled again.

"Why, what's going on?"

"The *Tokai-Kaibutsu* is angry." A gutter came loose from the wall just above where Blaine had stepped past and the boy turned his elfin face around in alarm. "We hurry. See, it changes." Kazuto pointed his finger towards an intersection of alleyways up ahead that, unbelievably, began to morph before Blaine's eyes. Where the alley had once stretched on past the crossroads it was now sealed over with cracking, green-tinged plaster as if it had never been. Blaine stood there with his mouth open but the boy had already begun to sprint. "Hurry!"

Blaine ran after him and this time when the walls began to seem as though they were closing in on him he realised that it was not an illusion. They really were shifting closer together. Adrenalin gave him another burst of speed and he followed the boy through a terrifying maze of walls and shadows that shifted and warped like smoke. It was as if the walls didn't want him to get where he was going; Blaine had no doubt that if they turned back the walls would let them through.

Eventually the boy came to a stop, Blaine nearly running into him from behind.

"Here," Kazuto said, his hand on the building beside him.

Blaine looked up and saw a building no different from any of the others – it was another forty-storied concrete monstrosity with that same green hue and faceless black mirror-windows.

"Go on then."

"No!" Kazuto looked genuinely frightened. "The *Tokai-Kaibutsu* is already angry with me."

"If you want your money you'll show me where in that building she is."

Lightening flashed in the distance but there was still no rain, yet.

"Okay-ey." The boy said desperately. He slipped through a gap in the wall that Blaine hadn't even noticed and the investigator followed.

Inside Blaine found himself in a shadowy corridor lit only by a flickering bulb at the far end. The carpet was mushy under his feet and he couldn't see enough to determine its colour. The walls were grey and grimy; the corridor was lined with small wooden doors. Rationally Blaine knew that people must exist behind those doors, that outside of this corridor Tokyo was moving towards midnight. Instinctively though he also knew that although there must be hundreds of people in this building he would see none, just as he hadn't seen another soul aside from Kazuto since the taxi had dropped him off. He followed the boy towards the end of the corridor and the lift that stood there. Blaine pushed the lift call button but Kazuto touched his arm when it arrived.

"See," Kazuto said, his eyes wide as he touched the wall beside the lift.

Blaine touched it too and felt the vibrations running through it. He realised he didn't want to get into the lift either.

"Come," Kazuto said, moving up the stairs to their left.

"What floor?"

"Twenty-four."

"Oh, hell." But Blaine followed him up the steep stairs anyway.

Twice the odd pair paused for breath before starting up again, and each time Blaine praised the Lord he'd kept himself fit over all these years. It seemed that every couple of levels the walls shook harder and from outside came the unmistakable sounds of thunder and lightening.

After another timeless interval composed of steps, panting and green shadows they reached the floor that made Kazuto's hand go up in a 'stop' motion. They halted, both breathing heavily and leaning against the wall of the stairwell. Blaine's breath was harsh and his legs were trembling. Grimly he fingered his holster underneath his t-shirt. He had survived worse than this in the war.

"Let's go," said Blaine firmly.

Kazuto nodded, his pupils very wide in the dim light. They started up the narrow corridor, the soles of Kazuto's sneakers flashing white in the darkness like matching bunny tails. The shaking of the floor had become worse, the floorboards rocking underneath the carpet like a ship in a rough sea. The single bulb by the lift was flickering wildly and the plaster on the walls was cracking off.

Kazuto stopped outside the fourth door on the left. "Here."

Blaine nodded and unholstered his gun. He had the most illogical idea that killing the girl would put an end to this madness. He motioned Kazuto to stand behind him and then he aimed a solid kick at the door. There was a small splintering noise and it swung open, easily. Blaine peered inside. The room appeared to be empty.

The girl's hideout consisted of a small bed-sit with two rooms: a cramped bedroom with a bed, desk and stove and an even tinier bathroom off to the right-hand side. The ceilings were slanted and all the furniture was covered in various items of clothing. Blaine stepped inside, the boy following, and instantly all the building's movements ceased. The floor stopped vibrating and the lights stopped flickering – a hush fell over the place and Blaine was so surprised he looked up and for just a moment his finger fell away from the trigger of his gun.

"Ahh!" A high scream came from somewhere behind him and a strong blow knocked Blaine's legs out from under him. His gun went flying and was snatched up quickly by his assailant.

Kazuto screamed too, a high pitched boyish sound that was suddenly cut off. Blaine scrambled to turn over on the floor and heard the unmistakable *snick* of the safety catch on his gun being taken off. He half-lay, half-sat on his back and raised his head slowly. Beatrice Eury was staring down at him over the barrel of his gun, her eyes glittering. Off to one side stood Kazuto, his hands clapped over his mouth.

"Careful now," Bunny's voice was low and husky. "No sudden movements." She continued to stare at Blaine even when she started talking to Kazuto. "Boy, you can go. But you better tell this story to all your friends."

"*Tokai-Kaibutsu?*" Kazuto whispered.

"Yeah."

"W-we say, it is no real."

"Not everyone says that."

"Only the street kids."

"But what are you going to say from now on?"

"Say *Tokai-Kaibutsu* real."

"Well done. Now scoot, before the *Tokai-Kaibutsu* gets really angry."

"I-I'm sorry." Kazuto darted out the door like a minnow.

"What is that word?" Blaine asked, his eyes fixed on the gun.

"Shut up. Give me a reason why I shouldn't just kill you."

Blaine hesitated. Unbidden, his memory recalled the other young woman who'd wanted to kill him. He shook away the memory – *she smiled underneath her veil of hair* – and looked up to see Bunny regarding him coldly.

She was wearing tight jeans with a wide leather belt and a black strapless top. Her jeans were rolled up to her knees and she stood barefoot. She wore no jewellery but her eyes were smudged with mascara again – her eyelids were rimmed with kohl and Blaine wondered if she'd just woken up. Her blond hair was loose in un-brushed ringlets that looped lazily around her face and down her shoulders. Her face was bone-white except for the two spots of pink staining her cheeks. Now that he could see her in better light Blaine appreciated how thin she really was – her collarbones looked so visible and delicate he wondered how they didn't just snap. The belt too was hitched on its smallest setting, judging by the amount of spare leather dangling at right angles from her hip. Her face was all planes and angles – no plumpness remained to soften it. Her eyes were wide but unlike last night there was no sign this time that she was spaced out, the green orbs were as focused and impenetrable as the black windowpanes in the city outside. Blaine saw that she held the gun in both hands and it didn't waver. He couldn't help but compare her to – *Lilly, with her red fingernails and long eyelashes* – that other woman. There was madness in both of them but they were of a very different type. The other woman had been crazed in a cruel, sexual way whereas this one seemed pushed to the edge of something. She was all stretched and taut. Blaine dropped his eyes from Bunny's and tried to think why she shouldn't kill him. Was there any reason, other than that he wanted to live? Eventually he raised his head and gave an answer more mundane than meaningful.

"Don't you want to know why I've been searching for you?"

"It doesn't take a genius to figure out."

"You don't even want to know who hired me?"

"I know who hired you." Her green eyes suddenly became distracted and her left hand played with a lock of hair.

"You do?"

"Of course." She actually sounded amused.

"I see. Is there anything you *do* need to know?"

Bunny opened her mouth to reply – Blaine saw her pink tongue and the tips of her front teeth – but then the earthquake exploded.

CHAPTER 7

The creature moved in the gloom, disturbed by the rumblings in its guts. It watched the motions in the bed-sit warily, the figures moving too quickly for it to catch nuances. Through the bottom of the bottle-green it recognised danger and sent quick tiny shivers to a deep, disused part of itself down under the surface. It turned back to worrying at the wound. Then, a few moments later, listened as somewhere far below in a place of green shadows tiny metal cogs began to squeak and whir, listened as a rusty old mechanism was called back into service…

* * *

The assault was the thing that drew Bunny and Blaine together. Probably nothing else would have.

It began with an earthquake, a tremor so violent it ripped through the tiny room in a tornado of cracking walls, circling dust and flying furniture. Bunny went flying too – she was lifted straight off her feet and sent headfirst into the ceiling before bouncing down like a rag doll onto the bed. The desk collapsed onto Blaine and the ancient blocky computer monitor toppled off the canted surface narrowly missing his head. The ceiling sloped and then cracked down the centre in a horrific creaking sound; dust and paper poured out of the crack and the steel beams that held the building together poked through into the room.

"It's Faber!" Bunny screamed, as one of the metal beams stabbed down inches away from where she lay on the mattress. Blaine couldn't see her clearly because of the dust and debris filling the air but he could hear her over the creaking of the joists even though his ears felt stuffed with cotton wool.

"Don't be daft," Blaine shouted as he pulled himself up off the now-slanted floor.

Bunny laughed – a wild high sound. She seemed to be scrabbling on the bed for something and Blaine realised she'd lost the gun. He reared up to grab her but blood obscured his vision and in a wave of dizziness he fell back to the floor. His eyes started streaming and they were hazed with red. Blaine wiped his hand across his forehead and it came away sticky. Damn. He heard sudden motion in the bed above him and a low keening started.

"Bunny?" The idea of being trapped alone in this haunted mausoleum was suddenly unbearable. The keening continued: a high, shrill sound more animal than human. "Are you okay?" There was no answer so with a wrench of will Blaine pulled himself up on the desk, his palms flat on the tilted surface and his biceps bulging with the strain. The expected wave of dizziness came and he hung onto the table like a drunken sailor.

"Bunny," Blaine croaked again.

"Oh, darling," came the whisper, in between low moans.

Blaine wiped his sleeve across his eyes and tried to blink away the blood and the dust. He could hardly see anything; only one bulb in the centre of the room was still lit and that flickered green. Bunny was lying on the bed with one leg bent at an awkward angle. Both of her hands were touching the nearest wall – in this case a block of plaster that had cracked and was leaning over her – and she seemed to be caressing it. Her palms and fingers were flat against the dirty surface and she was stroking the plaster urgently, her eyes closed as she mumbled to herself.

"It'll be all right, honey, really," she repeated in between hitched breaths. "It'll be fine."

Blaine seriously doubted at this point that anything was going to be all right but he planted his hands on either side of the bed and leant over Bunny anyway.

"You're right, it will be fine, honey." Blaine said thickly. "But we have to go now."

"No!" The sound was more a screech than a word. Bunny's eyes snapped wide open, the whites showing like in a feral dog. Her hands scrabbled beside her hip on the duvet and in a cry of pain she brought up the gun. She held it in both hands, the barrel only inches away from Blaine's face.

"Don't," said Blaine, quietly. A long moment passed. He could hear his own harsh breathing and his heart pounding in his chest. The girl was breathing in high, short gasps that bordered on squeaks. This time the gun shook in her hands. Blaine prayed she didn't pull the trigger by accident.

"Why?" she asked softly, the ruin of the room all around her.

"Because if you do you'll die here." Blaine looked down at the mess of her leg. One of the ceiling beams had stabbed down through her thigh, to just above her kneecap. It looked as if it had pierced the flesh straight through; there was a little blood soaking through her jeans but not much and that implied the metal was plugging the wound. Bunny followed his eyes but to her credit only blanched.

"I see," she whispered. "What are you proposing?"

"Put the gun down and I'll help you."

She laughed and the sound turned into a hacking wretch. The gun swayed wildly. "You were hired to kill me. If I put the gun down you'll do just that."

"Not right now. I need you."

"Why?" One of Bunny's hands left the gun and strayed towards the bulging wall, where she gently began to stroke it.

Blaine's eyes followed her fingers. "Because I'll never get out of this hell without you."

She smiled and the green light of the room reflected queerly in her eyes. "Sure you will. You just leave me here and walk out the room." Her tone betrayed the lie.

"No. You'll shoot me." He didn't add that he didn't want to be alone here, although he might have done. "And I don't understand this place. I don't think I'll get out without help."

The girl gave that strange, falling laugh again. "That much certainly is true."

"Come on," Blaine started to move closer to her but the gun was snapped back into his face.

"How do I know you won't kill me once I've led you outta here?"

Blaine shrugged. "You don't, really. But I'm a man of my word. I need you. And you need me."

The girl swallowed and then her head fell back onto a pile of clothes. "Okay," she breathed. It was as if the strength had all run out of her.

Her hand holding the gun fluttered to the bed and her face went an even lighter shade of white. Blaine took a step to the right to better evaluate her leg. The steel pylon was huge – as big as her thigh – but he realised when he got closer that its tip had split into two. The part that had gone through her leg was about the width of three fingers, the ends looked sharp and jagged. He prodded around on the mattress beneath her but it was as he'd feared - the steel had completely impaled her. Blaine sucked in air through his teeth and his large hands started to examine the ceiling where the beam had come through. The grey plaster had been sheared in two and it was cracking on either side of the steel. As he was examining it he heard the unmistakable sounds of footsteps pounding up stairs.

"You have to hurry!" Bunny's eyes were very wide in the dark. "Faber's men from last night!"

Blaine nodded wordlessly and applied his not inconsiderable strength to lifting the ceiling beam. Something popped in his back and his vision blurred again but he kept pushing upwards, his arms raised above his head in a Herculean effort. He gasped and sweat ran down his forehead and spine but it was not enough. The beam moved not an inch. Blaine dreaded to think of the weight pressing down on it from above. The whole building seemed to be subsiding. After a few moments Blaine stopped, panting. The footsteps were coming louder now – they could not be far off this floor.

"I'm sorry," he said hoarsely. "I need a saw."

"We don't have time. They'll kill you too."

"I know! But I can't lift this beam and I can't think of any other way to get you out. The bed's bolted to the floor."

"I don't have a saw."

Blaine swallowed at her flat tone and looked down at her. Bunny's green eyes were large and terrified. He'd left a man to die once in Yugoslavia. Her expression reminded him of that wounded soldier.

"It might be all right. We've got the gun."

She looked up in surprise, her face suddenly young and vulnerable. Then it closed off. "Wait," she murmured. "There might be another way." She shut her eyes and placed both palms flat on the wall again. Blaine saw his chance to grab the gun but what was the point? The gunmen would be here before he could escape. "Honey," the girl continued, "can you hear me? I need you."

There was a rumbling from the walls, a vibration that Blaine felt through the soles of his shoes. He could still hear the footsteps outside, winding up stairwells and growing close.

"Yes, I know," Bunny continued in a tone so soft her words all ran together. "I know it'll be bad. But it still has to be done. Please."

There was another moment of silence and then the ceiling began to shake violently. Bunny lay back on the bed with her eyes closed, her left hand on the wall. Her lips moved soundlessly. Her right hand was clenched over her chest, screwed up in the black fabric of her top.

And then the beam started to move. It went slowly at first, the great steel girder shuddering from side to side before it began to move upwards. Bunny whimpered but cut it short by stuffing her right hand in her mouth. Blaine put his hands on her leg around the wound to pin it to the bed, prevent it from lifting upwards on the beam. The metal moved creakingly, sliding out of her flesh inch by bloody inch. It seemed to be moving relatively easily until suddenly something snagged and Bunny screamed. Then the banging started at the door. Blaine met Bunny's eyes over the pale fist of her hand. At the other end of the room another piece of ceiling had collapsed to half-block the door. The beam above the bed had stopped moving.

"Come on!" Blaine punched at the ceiling with his fist and the girder started moving again. Bunny shrieked again and this time jammed both fists into her mouth; Blaine concentrated on guiding the beam out of her leg. The emerging metal was a gory sight - the steel was coated with blood and soggy bits of flesh. He was experiencing tunnel vision and his hands were slick with blood. There was the sound of gunfire behind him and he knew that someone was shooting at the lock. The last of the steel emerged from the leg with a jolt; the ends looked jagged and nasty. As soon as the tip left her skin blood spurted from the messy wound. Blaine couldn't see much of the wound itself – it was half covered by sodden jeans and bits of metal – but it looked as if her leg was still well attached. He slid his belt off and wrapped it tightly just above the gash then picked up the gun and turned to face the door. The falling sheet of plaster had prevented them from opening the door even though they'd shot the lock off. Blaine knew that his only chance of getting out of this netherworld alive was to shoot his way through the men and carry Bunny out of the building. He couldn't leave her behind – not only had he promised but also she seemed to be the only one who could navigate around the strangeness.

"No!" Bunny reached out a hand to touch his back from the bed behind him. "Not that way."

"Then what?"

"Pick me up."

"Bunny I can't shoot -"

"Trust me." Her voice was faint but sure.

Blaine gave Bunny the gun and kept one eye on the splintering door but did as asked and picked her up. He held her carefully in his arms, her right leg swinging loose like a broken doll's. He turned around so that she was facing the door, could point the gun at it, but she thumped him weakly in the chest.

"No," she croaked. "That way." She pointed to her right with the gun, towards the wreckage of a shelf that had fallen down from the cracked wall.

Behind them bullets were firing into the plaster blocking the door and breaking it up. Blaine moved her towards the wall, thinking as he did so how crazy this was, and she swapped the gun into her left hand and reached out with her right.

"Closer," she whispered. When her hand was flat against the plaster, the shots ceasing behind them as the first of the gunmen made it into the room, she murmured something else. She said: "Now don't let go."

And then her hand wasn't just stroking the plaster but *sinking* into it as if it were treacle. She reached out with both hands now, the gun tucked under one armpit, digging her nails into the wall and pulling Blaine with her into the malleable stone even as the gunshots slammed into the plaster left behind them.

Blaine found himself in a warm, cushy substance that was sort of like a black viscous fluid tinged with green. He looked down and saw that Bunny was still in his arms, still pulling her way through the stuff with her nails.

"Where are we?" he asked. His words had a slow, thick timbre to them that suggested sound didn't travel well here.

Bunny didn't turn her head but her words still came back clearly. "Somewhere we're not meant to be."

And then they were through. Air and light flooded back to Blaine and he coughed, loosing his footing. Bunny screamed as they fell, clutching at his chest in agony.

"It's okay," Blaine mumbled as he got up. "I'm sorry."

Bunny was gasping. "It's fine. But we have to be quick."

Blaine looked around. They seemed to be standing in another part of the building, in another identical corridor. The carpet was still dark and grimy and the walls were dirty with big cracks running through them. Blaine wonderingly turned his head to look at the wall behind them. It seemed as solid as ever.

"But surely they can't follow us?"

Bunny shook her head. "No. But we still have to be fast."

Blaine was ex-military. "Okay. Where?"

"That way, to start." Bunny pointed to one end of the corridor and Blaine carried her there.

At her instruction they travelled through the corridor, down one flight of stairs and to the end of another corridor. This time when Bunny reached for the grimy wallpaper Blaine was almost prepared for what came next. He once again erupted into thick dark fluid and this time the journey was longer. The silhouette-walls pulsed green around them and it felt distinctly as though he were moving through some deep oceanic trench.

When they emerged out at the other side they appeared to be in another building altogether. They were standing in a concrete, cavernous warehouse with high ceilings and plastic crates stacked around the walls. It was colder here but Blaine could no longer hear gunfire.

"What now?" he asked.

"We're in the next building, it'll buy us some time but we need to be fast. Do you have a car?"

"No." There was no time wait for a cab, either.

Blaine found himself looking down at her leg as he thought. Bunny followed his gaze – the stab wound felt wet and hot. Strangely her foot hurt more than the wound itself - the toes throbbed and sent shooting jets of pain up her calf. After looking at that she looked up at her rescuer – there was a wide gash just below his hairline and his face was smeared with blood and dust. His eyes shone very blue through the dirt.

"We need transport," Bunny said. "We have to get away from here."

"You couldn't just magic us away?"

"Not so far. Unless... Wait." Bunny cocked her head to one side. She seemed to be listening to something. "Down."

"What?"

"The stairs. Down. Are you okay to carry me?"

"Sure." Blaine hoisted her higher on his chest and set off again. It truly was no trouble, the girl was as light as a child.

Bunny directed them down seven flights of long, deep stairs and then they crossed another of the big warehouse spaces to a smaller staircase on the far side.

"The basement," she said breathlessly. The building seemed to shake a tiny bit, perhaps it was the aftershock of the earthquake.

"You sure?"

"Yeah. Down." Blaine followed her directions dutifully.

Once they reached the dark, dingy basement Blaine realised he could feel the walls vibrating again.

"Put me on the floor," Bunny whispered. Blaine cradled her gently to the ground but she still cried out when her lame leg hit the concrete.

"Hold onto me," she murmured after a few seconds. Her eyes were closed. "I've never done this before."

"Wha-" Blaine started, but it was already happening.

Unbidden, he felt his limbs melting through the floor. They were sucked into plasticine, gooey grey stuff that swallowed his hands and feet. This was worse somehow than moving through walls – at least you sometimes saw the latter in ghost movies. But moving through floors...

there was something fundamentally wrong with that. This time there was no 'space' to move through either; Blaine had the sensation of sinking into black water and then of rushing lights and movement. It was horrifying. And then they literally fell out of the ceiling onto something else. Bunny shrieked again as her leg hit the floor and Blaine banged his elbow on a metal railing. He looked around urgently. They had fallen into the middle of an aisle with double seats on either side and metal railings on the ceiling. There were doors at either end of the narrow room and dim lighting came from overhead. The walls were covered in windows and Blaine realised with a shock that the black streaks in them were a result of the fact the room was moving… they were on a subway train. Somewhere along the way Bunny had also lost hold of his expensive gun.

"Fuck!" Blaine swore. He looked around the carriage but the gun was nowhere to be seen. "What is this place?"

"It's been disused since the February earthquake."

"Then where the hell is it going? How is it running?"

Bunny ignore both his questions and when Blaine looked over at her he saw that she was as white as a sheet. Her leg was bent at an obscene angle beneath her.

He concentrated on the immediate. "Can they get to us here?"

"No." She was panting. "We'll be safe for a few hours."

Blaine looked up at the windows, at the lights that streaked past the glass. "And when we have to leave?"

"I don't know." She was a bad liar.

"You need a hospital."

"I'll live."

"You really might not." Brusquely Blaine turned away and began searching the luggage racks hanging above the train windows.

Bunny stared at his back. She was silent for a minute or so and the train chugged on. Then: "Who are you?"

Blaine gave a short laugh. "Funny to think I know so much about you but you don't even know my name."

"What is it?"

Blaine ceased his rummaging to turn and look at her. She looked tiny, crouched on the floor between the seats. The carriage rocked steadily from side to side and she hung onto one of the seats to try and prevent jolting her leg. She looked up at his scrutiny, her delicate features drawn with heavy charcoal lines. Her green eyes were wide.

"It's Blaine. But all you need to know about me is that I was paid to kill you."

"Then why did you help me escape?"

"Because if I hadn't have done we'd both be dead. You'd have shot me and they'd have shot you."

"So why not kill me now?" The trained shuddered under them.

"Because I want to know what's going on! You just pulled me through a wall. Through lots of walls! And now this… what the fuck is going on?"

"How much were you paid to kill me?"

"Half a million."

"Ah. And can I take it you're the one I have to thank for finding me?"

"Yeah."

"How?"

"I traced your laptop."

"Oh." Bunny breathed out with a long sigh and eased her body flat against the floor. The pain was turning into a red haze. "You cunning old bastard."

Blaine turned away, back to the luggage racks filled with litter and old coats. He tried hard not to think of Lilly. "You murdered your father. You don't deserve to hide away from that."

"Oh I *see*! So you're not really a hit man at all, more some sort of vigilante. Does that mean you're not just here to kill me for the money? Because I didn't kill my father."

"You're lying."

"Of course I'm not lying. What would be the point? I loved my father."

Blaine hesitated, caught by the real grief in her tone. "Where is this train going?"

"I don't know. You're avoiding the question."

"I'm here because you're a murderer! Killers like Lilly need to be stopped."

"Like who?"

"Like you."

"No, you said 'like Lilly'. Who's Lilly?"

"No one." Blaine wiped an arm across his face. "Look, how do I know you're telling the truth?"

"You have a direct line to Faber?"

"Yeah, why?"

"Give me the phone."

Blaine swallowed and after a moment drew his mobile out of his jeans. He dialled the number and threw it wordlessly to Bunny. She put the mobile on loudspeaker and then pressed 'call'. The dial tone rang out through the carriage.

"Any progress?" Faber asked as he picked up.

"Faber. You murdering bastard. Stop sending men to kill me."

There was an astonished silence. "You killed Mr O'Dwyer? I am impressed."

"You killed my father, you son of a bitch!"

"Now, now. You know that's not entirely true. I have people to do those things for me." Bunny looked as if she'd been punched. Into the silence, Faber continued. "You do know I'm going to kill you too, don't you? Your father was a fool to think you could just run off with his stolen goods into the sunset."

"You know *nothing* about my father."

Faber laughed, a rich sound that filled the subway car. "On the contrary, I know just as much as you do. You just don't want to admit the half of it. Carry on running, little bunny. You don't have long left." The line clicked and went dead.

After that the carriage was silent. Blaine stared at Bunny, feeling winded. His hands were closed tightly around a first aid box.

"Well?" Bunny stared up at him but the fire was draining from her eyes.

"I -" Blaine started, but then rushed forwards as Bunny's head fell forwards onto the seat in front of her.

All Machiavellian schemes forgotten, Blaine knelt beside her. "Come on, wake up."

"No. No more, no more..." her voice trailed off.

"I've got to do something about your leg. You're loosing too much blood." Blaine looked around the subway car and shivered. He couldn't imagine being stuck in this place alone. Not when she was the one with all the eldritch powers. He slapped her face gently. "Bunny! Wake up!"

"No," she murmured again. "No more."

Blaine took hold of her thigh and her kneecap and with a forceful *wrench* twisted them straight. Bunny screamed and shot up but he pinned her shoulders down.

"Shut up and listen to me." Blaine's blue eyes were cold as they drilled into her. As he spoke he pulled the belt off his jeans and wrapped it tightly just above the wound. "I need you alive. I don't know where the fuck we are! I need you. I need to patch up your leg."

Bunny listened silently, her nails digging into Blaine's wrist. She looked very young and vulnerable. Eventually she nodded and relaxed her grip. She put her head flat against the floor and grasped the metal frames of the bus seats on either side of her with both hands.

"Good." Blaine snapped open the first aid box and set to work.

He began by giving her a heavy dose of aspirin and then used the miniature scissions to cut open the jeans around the wound. The fabric was dark and stiff, glued to the flesh beneath. When he saw how filthy it all was he sat still for a few moments, making up his mind, and then retrieved the half-empty water bottle he'd seen jammed into the side of one of the seats. It wasn't sterile but it would be better than nothing. He poured the water all over the leg, watching it run off brown and bloody. As gently as he could he then wet a piece of his t-shirt and cleaned the edges of the wound. There wasn't too much fresh blood because the tourniquet was still wrapped tightly half-way up her thigh, like some bizarre garter, but enough dribbled out to make the job more difficult. Bunny stayed silent throughout and when Blaine looked at her he saw that she'd jammed one hand into her mouth and that tears were streaming behind her closed eyelids.

"You're doing well," he murmured, just to have something to say. "I'm gonna try and splint your leg now."

Blaine looked around for something he could use as a splint and eventually settled on an old umbrella. The cloth part was ripped where the broken spokes had poked through but that didn't matter. The old-style wooden handle was still attached. Blaine ripped the spokes off and eased the wooden stick beneath the girl's leg. Gently he loosened the belt and was gratified to see that not much fresh blood flowed.

"I'll need your belt too, I'm afraid."

Bunny nodded but made no move to take it off herself. Blaine unhooked it carefully and slid it out from around her waist. When he did so her trousers slipped down a little and he saw that she was wearing pale pink underwear. The colour captivated him for a second – it was the first bright colour he'd seen in a night of monochrome. As if in warning the bulbs in the carriage flickered and took on a greenish tinge. Blaine returned to the task at hand. He strapped the second belt to the umbrella just below her knee and tied it as tight as the first: hopefully tight enough to hold the leg still but not enough to restrict the blood flow. Then he set to work on the stab wound itself. The cut was surprisingly neat but it was deep and wide; it hadn't severed the tendons but it had crushed the bone. Blaine used the tube of superglue in the first aid box to glue the open flesh together. He could do nothing about the broken bone but straighten it. When he was finished he wrapped the whole thing together in bandages. It didn't look neat but it did look secure, no longer a fatal injury.

"Bunny," Blaine said, rocking her shoulder.

"Yes?" She didn't open her eyes.

"It's done for now. How long are we safe here for?"

"Hours. Sleep. Just a little. I need sleep." Bunny dropped back into unconsciousness. Perhaps the heavy dose of painkillers were having an effect. Blaine sighed but he, too, could no longer deny his exhaustion. His head wound was throbbing and he was sweating. His vision was blurring and he felt slightly sick. He lay down beside Bunny and shut his eyes just for a moment while the train rumbled on into the darkness.

When he awoke, nearly half an hour later, he had difficulty working out where he was. He was being rocked gently from side to side, his head resting on a hard surface. When he opened his eyes he saw that Bunny had moved a little way away from him on the floor, that her eyes were open and she was staring at him. She'd tied her hair back with something to reveal her tired, dirty face.

Blaine blinked away his grogginess and tried to form words. "Let's say you've convinced me you didn't kill your father. That still doesn't tell me what the fuck is going on here?"

"It's complicated," Bunny said warily. Just because the man seemed not to want to kill her anymore didn't mean she trusted him. She had no intention of telling him anything that Faber didn't already know.

"I don't care. Tell me something, anything. How do you do your moving through walls trick? How is this train moving? *Where are we going?*"

"Faber killed my father."

"I know. Why?"

"Because he knew things he shouldn't have done. The same things I know."

"And that's why he wants to kill you?"

"Yeah. Look. Faber's evil. With a capital 'E'. He won't... he'll do anything. He's quite mad."

"Why? Just because he killed your father?"

"Yes. No. No, more than that. Because he caused the earthquake tonight. And the one in February. He's evil. What he's doing, it's against nature."

Blaine felt lost. "I don't understand."

"You will." Bunny turned towards the rushing dark of the windows, a fey look in her eyes. "Just be quiet now. You're being taken into the centre of it."

The train rumbled on.

Over the next half hour Blaine sat silently in the corner. He was feeling sick again and his head was reeling. He kept having flashbacks - *Lilly on the first day they'd met with her sensible black heels, seeing the lipstick on the filters of her cigarettes, her black hair fanned out on the tiles and her blood* - he moaned softly and tried to push her away.

Bunny remained in her position on the floor, thinking equally dark but less confused thoughts. She had to go back to England now, didn't she? She had to end this now. She'd run and hid but if she wasn't safe here she wouldn't be safe anywhere. She'd run as far as she could and still Faber had found her. And things would be worse back in England, now. Now he'd found her where she was. She had to go back.

After a while underneath the flickering lights of the subway tunnel the train began to slow and eventually stopped.

Blaine looked up. "Where are we?"

Bunny put out her hand, taking pity on him. "Help me up. I want to show you something."

Horribly confused, Blaine helped her up and he half-walked, half-carried her to the train door set into the left side of the carriage. Part of the glass door was smashed but it still *whooshed* open as they approached.

Outside the train lay a wrecked subway platform, the underground hollow caved in and full of rubble and bent steel. It was deathly quiet and lit only by one dim bulb hanging above a broken sign.

"Where are we?" Blaine found himself whispering.

"Near the centre of the last earthquake." Bunny also whispered, even as she instructed Blaine to walk them both to the far end of the platform. The south end was shrouded in darkness. "Many people died here. The street children whisper that it was the wrath of the *Tokai-Kaibutsu*."

"What does that mean?"

Bunny shot him a look, not dissimilar to the one Blaine had received from Kazuto the night before. "It is hard to explain." She put a finger to her lips.

Together they approached the black shadows that curved over the end of the platform. Rubble moved beneath Blaine's feet and his pupils grew wide as they accustomed themselves to the pitch black.

"There," Bunny whispered, pointing with her right hand.

Blaine strained his eyes and saw only light reflecting off a few dust motes hanging in the air. He opened his mouth to question, then closed it again as he realised that it was not just dust that hung there suspended in nothingness. Along with slivers of rock and splinters of steel hung a little silver spoon, sparkling in the darkness.

"My God," he murmured. "What is that?"

"It is a scar on the face of the world. A breach of the laws of physics. It is -"

"It's unholy."

Bunny drew a deep breath. "Yes."

"And you say that Faber did this."

"Yes."

Blaine turned to face her. He felt the wrongness of this place in his very bones – it was a discord in the fabric of everything. "I want to help you. I want to stop him."

Bunny laughed. The noise was loud in this place; the high sound echoed strangely through the fallen tunnel. A little dust spiralled down from the domed ceiling. "What makes you think I'm going to stop him?"

"What you said on the phone. You're tired of hiding now."

Bunny tilted her head up to look Blaine in the eye. She looked very pale in the wreckage of the subway. "I don't trust you."

"That's fine. You don't have to. Just let me help."

"This is madness."

"No. It's not." Blaine struggled for words. "Look, I did something wrong, something awful, three years ago. When Faber offered me the chance to kill another murderess I thought... I felt it might be a shot at redemption. I know, it's mad. But I did. But it wasn't, it's just further down the same path, and now... This I know is wrong. I can see it. I can fight it. I want to." He was faintly aware he'd just made a speech. He repeated: "This is unholy."

Bunny swallowed, looking into his very blue eyes. "Okay," she said softly. And that seemed to be it.

The two of them walked back onto the subway train, which magically started moving as soon as they were both onboard.

The rest was surprisingly easy. The subway car ran for another twenty minutes, dim lights shooting past its windows, and eventually came to a stop in some demolished area of track. It seemed to be as far as it could go and when they got out they saw why: a rock fall had totally blocked the tunnel.

Silently Bunny motioned to Blaine to get off and follow her and although there was no platform here there was just room enough in the tunnel for them to get out of the train and stand.

"This way," she said authoritatively, pointing towards the blocked tunnel.

Blaine followed obediently. Dusty rock and broken glass crunched underfoot as the pair made their way towards the blockage at the end of the cavern. There was no light here except that which came from the dim bulbs inside the train carriages. When they reached the rockslide Bunny began climbing up it on her hands and knees and Blaine clambered up beside her. She favoured her injured leg and occasionally whimpered as she had to bend it awkwardly but made no other complaint. They were panting lightly by the time they'd reached the rocks that lay nearest the roof of the tunnel and when they reached the highest point Blaine saw that there was a hole in the ceiling.

"There?" he asked.

"Yeah. The subway dropped us off at its shallowest point. We'll have to do some more climbing, but it shouldn't be that far to the surface."

"Okay." Blaine continued to climb.

They scrambled up over the rocks that passed the height of the subway tunnel and began climbing up inside a fissure in the stone that was lined with bricks and earth. It wasn't too steep and they would have been able to make quick progress if there had been any light. As it was it was pitch black and they had to proceed slowly, until Blaine bumped his head on a hard ceiling of stone and earth. It seemed to be where the fissure stopped.

"Come here," Bunny said.

She grasped Blaine's hand and without another word *pulled* them up through the pavement and onto the street. Blaine's submergence in the toffee-like substance was quick this time and he burst onto the ground coughing and gasping, like he'd just been dunked underwater.

"You could've warned me," Blaine growled, as he looked around.

Bunny ignored Blaine's reproach and started walking down the road. They were back somewhere on the streets of Tokyo; a dim streetlight shone greenly on the other side of the road. The city appeared deserted and there were no other lights.

"Where are we going?" Blaine asked, falling into step beside her.

"Anywhere we can get a taxi from." Bunny's face was smeared with grime and she was beginning to limp heavily. Blaine wondered if the painkillers were wearing off.

After about twenty minutes of walking they reached a street that was more brightly lit than the others and ten minutes after that they reached a road that actually had traffic on. Blaine stuck out a thumb and the second taxi that passed pulled up beside them. As they slid onto the backseat Bunny spoke again. "So, you've got your passport right?"

"I always carry it with me when I'm abroad." A pause. "Do you have yours?"

"Kinda."

"It's a fake?"

"Yeah."

Blaine looked at her curiously. "So how did you get it?"

A grimace passed over Bunny's face. "My father got it for me before he died."

Blaine shot a look at her but said no more.

Four hours later they were sitting in two First Class seats on a direct British Airways flight to London. Blaine had paid for the tickets and was grateful for the fact he kept his wallet as well as his passport with him at all times. He was sad he was leaving his laptop behind in the grimy hotel but there was nothing he could do about it. While they were waiting in the queue he'd asked Bunny curiously where she'd got the money to live on during her time in Tokyo. She had replied demurely that the city had provided. They were both exhausted but had cleaned themselves up in the airport toilets with two packets of wet wipes and in one of the Departures shops Blaine had purchased Bunny a long skirt to hide her injured leg under. Her jeans were wrecked anyway and while there was no masking the terrible limp they could at least conceal the splint. On the plane, in the wide comfy seats, Blaine could almost imagine that the events of the last twenty-four hours hadn't happened. Then he'd look over at the ghostly, wan woman sitting next to him and reconsider.

As the plane took off Blaine thought he was leaving behind the high-rise, dirty city of Tokyo with its green shadows behind forever. And in a way he was quite right. But, in another way, he was quite wrong.

CHAPTER 8

Gideon leaned back in his executive leather chair and sighed to himself. His private mobile was sitting on the desk in front of him and stubbornly not ringing. He willed it to ring. He was mentally and physically exhausted. Using *it* always left him so. But sadly it was a necessity. He'd hired six hitmen in Tokyo for Christ's sake – not including the rouge Irishman – and so far they'd been chasing her for the last forty-eight hours with no success. So, to be sure, he'd taken extra measures.

Once he knew the exact location of her hideout causing the earthquake had seemed the logical thing to do. But now Gideon was urgently awaiting the call from the men he'd sent in after it, to confirm that Beatrice Eury was dead. He hadn't bothered to call Blaine; Gideon had held high hopes for the man after he'd tracked her to Japan but since then he had failed dismally. He'd spent hundreds of thousands trying to trace Bunny before he'd resorted to the ignominy of hiring a private detective and then to his surprise within a day Blaine had discovered her location. If he had somehow traced her flat and been killed in the earthquake it was just bad luck.

With another deep breath Gideon pressed the intercom on his desk and wandered over to the high windows with their magnificent views out onto the city. His PA took an inordinately long time to reach his office and Gideon occupied himself by gazing out over the roofs and people of London. Although he would never admit it aloud Gideon was aware that he was lonely. Part of him craved his three office suite back in the lower part of London, with its cramped waiting room, sulky receptionist and tiny white-walled office with the requisite leather couch. That place seemed like such an ancient memory, so distant it might have happened to someone else, but it wasn't yet a year ago. Gideon pressed his fingers against the windows - as if he could touch the past with his fingertips - then turned round guiltily when his PA appeared at the door.

"What can I do for you, doctor?" Fiona said.

She was pretty and efficient in a serious, list-making sort of way. Gideon had never slept with her although he vaguely entertained the idea from time to time. In all fairness Fiona had never seemed interested either; he wondered if she was married. She'd worked here for four months and he'd never asked.

"Some food, please," Gideon replied. It was nearly 4:00pm, that dead time between lunch and dinner, but he ate so little that it wasn't as if he was snacking between meals.

"And some tonic water?"

"Yes. That's all."

Fiona nodded and closed the door as she left with a soft *snick* behind her. Gideon returned to pacing in front of the window. When he'd decorated this room, with its oak bookshelves and grand desk, it had seemed minimalist and regal. Now it seemed austere and bare. How was it he'd come to spend all of his life in a room so featureless?

The sudden shrilling of his mobile broke him out of his reverie. Gideon leaped over to the desk and pushed the green 'accept' button.

"Yes?"

"Dr Faber." The caller's Japanese accent distorted the words, turned them into something like 'Dac-ter Fay-bure'.

"I have bad news. When we were attacking the building there was an earthquake and the girl ran away. My men chasing her now."

Gideon snarled down the phone. "How?"

"She had help. A white man was in flat with her. The earthquake demolished the walls and they ran."

"A man? What man?"

"White, dark hair, tall. He seem to be carrying her. We track them now."

"They've gone through the walls too?"

"Ah, no. More debris followed and that route is blocked. My men track other means."

"I see." Gideon sat back in his chair, his colour draining underneath his tan. A surreal, frightening scenario was starting to play out before his eyes. "Are they having any luck?"

"They still chase."

"Well, keep me informed." Gideon hung up and tried to breathe calmly. It was starting to look more and more as though he'd been betrayed. And yet surely that wasn't possible! Was it?

Gideon remembered when he'd first met his special patient, after that conference in Tokyo last year. His parents had been so worried, his psychiatrist so bumbling. Gideon been sceptical at first, of course, but after spending over three hours with the boy he'd become convinced. In order to try everything Gideon needed to take him to England. He'd kept in touch with the boy's parents, tried to monitor his progress over the following months and made several trips, and in the meantime Gideon made his preparations. The first time had been a disaster. An event that was supposed to call his patient to him, like a mentor to an extremely gifted student, had instead driven him away. When his parents had lost their son in the earthquake they'd searched for him valiantly and eventually grieved terribly when they finally gave him up for dead. Gideon though had known differently: his patient might be lost somewhere in the city but he was still alive, he wasn't someone who could die so easily. He tapped his fingers on the desk. Or, at least, he had thought so until recently. But now he was beginning to guess the truth, or perhaps just the shape of the truth.

And that was when the second phone call came.

After the conversation with Bunny Gideon was filled with rage and had to resist the urge to throw things. Instead, he pushed the intercom on his desk. How the devil had she managed to kill Blaine?

The intercom squawked its readiness.

"Fiona, I need to go back to Pottersby."

Despite the fact his request was unusual it was organised quickly. Fiona was nothing if not organised. A car was rung for and Gideon's big bodyguard Eluf was enlisted as driver. The only thing Gideon couldn't get out of was a board meeting by conference call at 4:30pm. He took it in the boardroom on the floor below his private office, sitting alone in the large panelled room. This one also featured large windows, with a print of London in the 1950s on the wall. He felt very alone, despite the huge video-screen projecting the other board members in New York. Gideon was the only British shareholder and that had used to be a source of pride. Now he just felt small and frightened. The only person who could take all of this away from him had just called him on his private mobile and called him a son of a bitch.

"So," continued Mr Sandwell, "we're agreed that in the event of the assets of Cell AN being exhausted we'll look to the insurance captive? We're all happy to sign a management agreement to that effect?"

"Yes," said Mr Cruyen.

"Yes," said Ms Jenner.

Gideon breathed out heavily through his nose. "Yes."

He hated this stuff, hated the day-to-day routine of the business empire he'd built for himself. He longed for the days of practising psychiatry in his little cramped office. He didn't seem to do any psychiatry any more. Now he spent his days on one long gravy train of board meetings and shareholder meetings and stock checks. He signed off this meeting early; he just couldn't cope with it anymore.

After the curtailed meeting Gideon instructed Eluf to drive him back to his townhouse before making the journey to Pottersby. The journey from the office took around twenty minutes but they eventually pulled up outside a large detached Victorian building insulated from the traffic-buzz of London. It was situated in Chelsea and had cost over two million; in addition to its six bedrooms it boasted a gym and a swimming pool. Gideon lived here alone, aside from the help. His car crunched on the gravel drive and Eluf slid out from the driver's side to open the front door. Gideon stepped into the high-ceilinged doorway, brightly lit by the chandeliers hanging overhead. It was beautifully decorated, down to the tasteful wallpaper and cream carpets, but it was also very formal and felt slightly unlived in. Gideon moved deeper into the property, running his fingers over the antique furniture and the pictures hanging on the walls. Upstairs he heard the noise of Eluf instructing a maid to pack bags for them. He moved into the larger of the two lounges, taking in the forty-eight inch widescreen TV and the curved cream sofas. Low coffee tables adorned the room but nothing rested on them. Except on one.

Gideon moved towards the coffee table that stood beside the large sash windows that led out onto the garden and picked up the solitary photo frame that stood on it. A woman smiled out of the expensive silver surround, her white teeth glinting in an unseen sun. She was olive-skinned and brown eyed with a glorious nimbus of brown curly hair that stood out around her head. She had been thirty-six when the photograph was taken, small crows-feet starting to show around her eyes and the hint of chubbiness in her neck and cheeks. The picture was yellowed with age: it was nine years old. This had been Gideon's life, before she'd left him for another man. The conversation replayed in Gideon's head as if it were yesterday.

"I want children, Gideon, and that's the end of it."

"You know I can't give you that." The knowledge of his infertility still rankled.

"Then adopt!"

"Here, now?" Gideon had waved his arm around their cramped apartment. *"If you wait for the perfect time and place you'll be waiting forever."*
"That's not true."
"If you don't then I'm leaving."

And she had. She'd been killed with her new husband and unborn child a year later in a car crash. It was then that Gideon's heart had begun its spiral into dark.

"Come on!" Gideon called to Eluf. "Let's get out of here."

The drive out of London was slow but uneventful and it speeded up quickly once they got onto the M40. Gideon reclined in comfort in the back of his Mercedes whilst Eluf did the driving. Autumn was nearly over and as the leaves fell from the trees lining the roads, all copper and gold, it became obvious that winter was setting in. Gideon leaned back and watched the leaves float gently from the trees as he travelled in style down the roads of rural England.

Once they reached Wolverhampton, just before they were due to leave the main roads altogether, Gideon made Eluf stop at a supermarket to buy groceries. Rosa wouldn't be expecting them as the cottage had no phone and Gideon would want something to eat when they arrived at their destination. After Eluf had collected the groceries Gideon reflected on that: how backwards it seemed now not to have a telephone line! But the house was so remote there was no way of fitting one. You couldn't even get a mobile signal out there – the only way Gideon was able to make calls was by getting Eluf to erect a radio mast on an extendable, plastic stick and connect the mobile up to it. It had driven Gideon mad the last time he'd stayed there but there seemed to be no alternative.

The last part of the drive to Pottersby was awkward because of the tiny roads but it was nonetheless beautiful: all the fields were draped in autumn and they were surrounded by sun-dappled trees. The walk to the cottage was, as ever, unpleasant but it was a necessary evil. When they walked past the forest shrine Gideon stared into it but there was no hint of the body that had once hung there. After nearly half an hour of trekking along the muddy dirt path the trees opened out a bit and he saw the thatched roof of Robert's old cottage poking out underneath an evening patch of pale pink sky.

When Gideon reached the front door the nurse came out. Even though it was past 8:30pm she made no comment on his unexpected arrival. Rosa was a petite Spanish woman whose work visa had expired; Gideon had hired her not only because she was a good nurse but also because he knew he had a hold over her.

"Any change?" Gideon asked hopefully.

Rosa shook her head. "No sir."

Gideon sighed. "Let me see him."

Rosa led him inside the house, her sensible brown bun bobbing behind her. She was in her mid-fifties and scurried rather than walked - she always put Gideon in mind of a squirrel. Inside the door opened out into a spacious hallway, the kitchen and lounge led off to the left and a study and library to the right. A small toilet was tucked underneath the stairs that led directly up to the two bedrooms and the only proper bathroom. All the ceilings were low and supported by oak beams that jutted out of the plaster. The walls were mainly painted a pale, creamy yellow that nicely offset the beams. Far from looking chocolate-box this modern touch merely emphasised the age of the cottage - history seemed to seep out of its walls. When he was here Gideon always felt very aware of the house, he felt as though it brooded in the background. He followed Rosa up the stairs and into the bedroom on the left side of the house. This room was decorated in a brighter yellow and many of the walls were low where they met with the white painted ceilings. The beams in the room were made of oak but the floorboards were pine. There was a print of Monet's *Rouen Cathedral* on one wall and a low chest stored against another but the focus of the room was on the double bed. It stood in the centre of the room, pushed back against the right hand wall, so that its occupant could see out of the skylights that ran parallel to the beams in the ceiling. Through the skylights the occupant could see the forest – all green branches and leafy shadows. At least, the occupant would see them if he opened his eyes to look.

The patient lay in the bed with his eyes closed, as he had since the last time Gideon had seen him. He appeared unchanged. His brown hair had grown down to his ears but it had been neatly combed. Blankets were tucked around his frail body and they were blue, the colour a boy might like. His expression was serene and his breathing was slow but light: he appeared to be sleeping peacefully.

Gideon turned to Rosa, who hung nervously in the doorway. "And he's been like this since I left?"

"Yes."

"He still eats?"

"Yes… I feed him soup, bathe him and take him to toilet. He is very light."

Gideon nodded. In this light-filled room his rushing down here seemed a little ridiculous. What he had feared was happening could not possibly be happening. "I'll stay tonight, and leave in the morning."

Rosa nodded and bustled off, probably to make more beds. Gideon would have the master bedroom but she and Eluf would have to sleep in the lounge or the library.

After inspecting his patient it was nearly 9:00pm and Gideon roamed about downstairs while Rosa cooked them dinner. She had clucked approvingly at Eluf's grocery shopping, unpacking the fresh milk, eggs, tomatoes, potatoes, bacon and sausages with obvious relish. The kitchen cupboards were already full of tinned goods but the fridge and fruit bowl were bare. The nearest food shop was the post office/general store in the hamlet and that was not only a few hours walk away but fairly ill stocked.

Gideon felt proud of his foresight in bringing food as he looked around Robert's library. The 'library' wasn't really a room in its own right but rather an awkwardly sized alcove in the strangely shaped study. In the neatly kept lounge there were some fiction novels but this study was devoted wholly to Robert's work. The study was lovely, an old man's room with the bare floorboards covered by a dark oriental rug and the walls painted a matching dusky red. A huge antique desk dominated the room; it was made out of oak with lots of drawers and books stacked on top of it. It looked a little like Gideon's desk except that the contents of this were far messier and adorned with little nicks and scratches. It looked well used and well loved, as did the massive antique swivel chair standing in front of it. The chair's five feet stood in a neat circle and the leather seat with its wide cushion and high, red back swivelled on them. The desk sat underneath a wide window that looked out of the east side of the house into the forest. The window had no curtains and all the rooms were dotted with table lamps. God only knew when the house had been fitted with its little electric generator – the rumbling machine was ancient and Gideon often worried that it would break down.

This evening Gideon circled the study, peering at the desk and out the window. He didn't sit in the chair. The bookshelves were of the most interest to him. He recognised some of the leather-bound hardbacks, such as Plato's *Republic*, Locke's *Study of Human Nature* and Kant's *Critique of Pure Reason*. Gideon had read little philosophy but he knew enough about it to recognise the classics. The rest of the books represented a glimpse into a different world: Chalmers' *The Conscious Mind*, Quine's *From a Logical Point of View*, Dennett's *Brainchildren*. There were also several shelves of journals. Faber picked up an issue of *Ratio* from 1993 and flicked to the contents page. The third paper featured was entitled "Why There Is No Glitter On the Brain"; it was described as 'a critique of epiphenomenalism' and was written by Professor Robert Eury. Gideon smiled to himself – the man obviously collected his own papers. Further down on the same shelf he found a first edition of Eury's *Emerging From Materialism*, the book that had cemented Robert's reputation as a metaphysician to be reckoned with.

Gideon put the book down and walked back through the lounge into the kitchen. His eyes moved over the cream ceramic sink, the old-fashioned stove with its thin patina of grease and the scrubbed worktops. On the windowsill above the sink were about a dozen small terracotta pots containing little violet flowers and herbs. The flagstones that made up the floor were neatly swept and saucepans were arranged in order of size on large hooks by the door. Rosa had taken some of the saucepans down to prepare a sausage casserole.

"It's nearly done," she said with a smile.

"Thanks," replied Gideon. He went to the drawers and began laying out the cutlery on the kitchen table. "Where's Eluf?"

"The woodshed. The season is turning. It will be cold tonight."

After a filling dinner of casserole and mashed potatoes, which the three of them ate in silence, Gideon went to bed.

Gideon's sleep was undisturbed that night but he awoke the next morning in a state of profound unease. The birds were tweeting outside the skylights in the master bedroom. He supposed that a different person might have found them quaint but he found it an intrusion, a reminder of how close to nature he was. This room was larger than the one across the hall, with the bed facing out onto the huge windows that stretched across the walls and up the ceilings. The blinds were drawn but the autumn sunlight still filtered through around the edges, casting dappled gold shadows of the leaves outside. Gideon stared at the patterns for a while then eased his tired body out of bed. This bedroom had belonged to Robert – his socks were still in the chest of drawers and a dog-eared copy of Hume's *Treatise* lay on the bedside cabinet. Gideon still felt sad that he'd had to kill the old man. He felt no such remorse about Bunny – she had never been useful to him. Gideon sighed as he pulled his creaking legs out of the sheets and dressed on the cold floorboards. He wished he could just magically make her disappear so that he could settle down to enjoy the fruits of his ingenuity. Who else, after all, what have thought to have done what he'd done?

After visiting the bathroom Gideon plodded down the steep, curving stairs and then called for Rosa. She came running at once, fully dressed with her hair already twisted into its neat bun.

"Yes sir?"

"Some breakfast, please."

"Yes sir. I've baked some bread and you could have it with some eggs or bacon?"

"Scrambled eggs would be great, thanks."

"No problem." Rosa bustled away and Gideon settled himself at the kitchen table.

It was odd but strangely pleasant not to be greeted by the morning papers and stock reports. There was no sign of Eluf yet and nothing else to think about except the events transpiring in Tokyo. What had happened in that hotel room, that Bunny had escaped and killed Blaine? Gideon assumed that she must have killed him – he couldn't see how else she would have acquired the Irishman's mobile. And she hadn't denied it on the phone yesterday. It must have been Blaine that the Japanese hitmen had seen in the flat, too. It was too much of a coincidence to assume that there were two black-haired Caucasian men running round in that part of the city.

As Rosa placed his breakfast in front of him Gideon began to get more worried. Just what *was* the girl doing? He tucked into his nicely seasoned eggs on a bed of fresh basil and tried to enjoy the country cooking even as his mind raced ahead to map the possibilities. What he had feared might have happened – the reason for which he'd come rushing down here – had not seemed to have happened at all. The patient was as comatose as he'd been two weeks ago when Gideon had last been down to check on him.

Gideon smiled and thanked Rosa courteously when she cleared his plate. Afterwards he even asked her to sit down with him once she'd made the coffee. They didn't really talk - what would they say to each other, after all? – but Gideon could tell she was glad of the companionship. It couldn't be much fun living here alone in a forest-bound cottage with only a sleeping beauty to keep her company. She couldn't even go into the hamlet to shop - Gideon couldn't let anyone know they were illegally occupying this place. Even though Robert's daughter was wanted for arrest the cottage still legally belonged to her.

As Gideon was draining the dregs of his coffee mug Eluf came in. His hair was damp and Gideon surmised that he must have gone for a run before having a shower.

"Eluf, I'm glad you're here. I intend to leave by mid-morning, but first

I'd like you to set up the telephone mast to see if there are any messages."

Eluf nodded and turned back out of the kitchen. He was a taciturn man but very loyal and capable. He'd been one of Gideon's first patients when he was a boy and Gideon was a newly qualified psychiatrist. He'd been brought to Gideon on the grounds that he was 'slow'; Gideon had diagnosed him with dyslexia. In those days dyslexia was a poorly understood and often mismanaged disorder but Gideon had shown the boy patience and with great care taught him how to deal with it. As the boy grew up he developed an almost pathetic affection for his doctor and so when Eluf's more violent urges had begun to show themselves Gideon had been on hand to show him how to manage and conceal that condition, too. The grown man made an unstinting bodyguard and loyal, if silent, companion. Gideon doubted Eluf understood what it was his beloved doctor had done to his special patient upstairs but he knew it wouldn't matter even if he did. And Eluf had skills that Gideon simply lacked; on that nasty night when Robert had died it had been Eluf who'd cleared up the mess and Eluf who'd so inventively arranged the body in the shrine. Once they had discovered that all notes of the experiment were gone it hadn't taken much detective work to realise that Robert had sent them to his only child. It also had not taken a genius to figure out that the child would be coming here. Eluf had suggested laying out the body in the shrine so that the girl wouldn't get as far as the house and Gideon had agreed. It was a masterly plan and should have worked flawlessly... except that Gideon had lost control. Control was the key to everything, he was discovering.

Ten minutes later Eluf shouted through the kitchen window that he was ready in the garden outside. Gideon opened the backdoor from the kitchen and stepped out onto the little patio. A small seating area was paved with heavy, mismatched flagstones and a low stone wall surrounded it. Flowers were planted below and above the wall and a rusty garden table with two chairs stood nearby. The white paint was flaking off the chairs and small shrubs were creeping up amongst the flowers. The whole area surrounding the patio was made of up of tall trees, so that sunlight was forced to filter down through the various varieties of leaves. Many of the leaves were yellow and red and they fluttered to the ground even as Gideon watched. It was a chilly day but a light one - no rain threatened yet. Eluf held out the control for the portable mast and Gideon attached his mobile to it. After thirty seconds or so the phone registered a signal. There were three new voicemails. Gideon pulled up one of the chairs while Eluf fiddled with the phone and put it on loudspeaker. Rosa went back into the cottage and began preparing porridge for her patient.

The first message was from Gideon's PA, telling him that some of his shares were looking as though they would shortly decrease in value and so did he want to sell. The second message was from one of Gideon's research specialists telling him that he'd found a new company producing innovative-looking drugs that could be useful in prolonging artificial foetal development. The third message was the frightening one. One of Gideon's contacts claimed that they had seen a 'possible sighting' of Beatrice Eury at Heathrow. Gideon's head snapped up when that information was played over the speakers.

"At Heathrow?" he repeated. "That's not possible."

Eluf shrugged and Gideon instructed him to call the man and get some details. Surely, surely, Bunny could not be in London. If she was it would mean that she'd gotten on a flight only a few hours after the earthquake… and she had no passport. But, Gideon reminded himself, she'd had no passport on the way out either and she'd still managed to leave the country.

Gideon went into the house and paced the small lounge while waiting for Eluf. Eventually the wait became too much and he stalked out into the garden where Eluf was just hanging up the phone.

"Well?"

"The man is fairly certain that it was Beatrice Eury, although he said that the woman walked with a heavy limp. He took a photograph but it shows only the side of her head so we can't be sure."

"Did he follow her?"

"No."

Gideon damned airport security guards and their lack of initiative. "But he does think it was her?"

"Yes."

Gideon pushed a hand through his thinning hair. "She's coming here."

Eluf looked uncomfortable. "We don't know that."

"I do. She's coming here." Gideon swallowed. "Get my equipment out of the car."

"Sir," Eluf looked pained. He hated to see the doctor use that *thing* on himself. "Even if she is coming here, we could alert the police, make it hard for her to get here."

"Oh yes. We'll make it as hard as humanely possible for her to get here." Gideon caught Eluf's eye and laughed. "And I don't just mean the police! She's shown that she's too resourceful just to be stopped by a couple of coppers. I have… other things in mind."

"Yes sir."

"And when you've been to the car you'll have to go get some more supplies, as well. We're going to stay here until it's over."

Eluf nodded sadly and set off briskly down the muddy path to the clearing where the car was parked.

Upstairs, in cottage's smallest bedroom that held all the skylights, the unconscious patient was spoon-fed lumps of creamy porridge like a sleepwalker while he dreamed and dreamed.

CHAPTER 9

Blaine breathed a sigh of relief when the wheels of the plane touched down on Heathrow runway. He looked over at Bunny and touched her hand. Her face was bone white and her legs were stretched at an awkward angle. Over the twelve hour flight she had become withdrawn and subdued, eventually lapsing into unconsciousness. Blaine was anxious to get her out of the airport – he didn't want her collapsing in Arrivals and drawing attention to herself. Thankfully Bunny stirred when he took her arm and her eyes opened. Wordlessly she unbelted her seatbelt and waited for the plane to come to a halt so that its passengers could disembark. When the seatbelt sign *dinged* off she stood up slowly and moved into the aisle with everyone else. Blaine followed her warily down the plane then onto the portable tube connecting the aircraft to the airport. He was glad they hadn't had to get off using the stairs. He stood beside her as they waited in the queue for Passport Control and when he noticed her lurching to the right he moved to her other side and let her lean on him. Bunny didn't speak or look at him; her jaw was clenched shut and two rosy spots had appeared high on her ashen cheeks. When they reached the checkpoint the guard merely glanced at their passports before waving them through. Blaine wondered if Bunny's use of fake a ID would be so easy if she wasn't Caucasian.

Once they'd passed Passport Control they moved quickly past baggage collection and into Arrivals. Their flight had left Tokyo at 6:00am on Monday morning and with the time difference they had arrived in London at 10:00am. There were signs for fireworks pasted all over the airport and Blaine realised with a shock that it was Bonfire Night tonight. Pulling himself back to the task at hand, Blaine supported Bunny by the elbow as he quickly escorted her past the ranks of taxi touts and waiting relatives. He wondered briefly about the wisdom of returning to his own car but quickly rejected his qualms: not only was it unlikely Faber would suspect enough to track it but he also wanted the spare guns stored in the boot.

"Over here," he said, pointing to the sign for long-term parking.

"Not my car."

"No, mine." Blaine re-gripped her arm and led her quickly through the concrete maze.

"You have the ticket?" Bunny asked.

"Yeah. I always leave it in the car."

Bunny nodded, her movements obviously becoming stiffer.

Eventually they came out into the long-term parking bays and Blaine guided them to his convertible. He unlocked it with a press of his key remote and then held the passenger door open for Bunny.

"Get in," he said gruffly. "I'll do the ticket."

Bunny smiled wanly. "Your car's much nicer than mine."

Blaine didn't reply but concerned himself with leaning over her to rummage in the glove box for the ticket. "Stay here."

He shut Bunny's door and went off to find a parking payment machine. The bill came to a whopping £76.50 for five days. Blaine stuck it on his Visa.

When he returned to the car he saw that Bunny was already asleep again; she'd positioned her splinted leg straight out in front of her in the foot-well by moving the seat back as far as it would go. Her eyes were shut and her head was tilted back against the headrest. Blaine got into the driver's side and started the car with a purr. He carefully reversed out of the parking bay and drove to the exit. It was a grey day outside and the natural light made Bunny look even paler. Blaine stuck his ticket into the machine's validating slot and after a few seconds the metal bar raised up to let the car through. It was only after he'd navigated his way out of the airport and onto the M25 that he realised he had no idea where he was going. He looked over at Bunny – she was so still she mightn't be breathing. With a roar Blaine brought the engine up to speed and careered off at 80mph towards the sign for the next motorway services. They appeared soon after on his left: a squat, ugly complex consisting of a Little Chef, a McDonalds and a Travelodge. Blaine pulled into the Little Chef car park and gazed up at the flickering image of the fat white chef in his red apron while trying to think.

"Bunny, wake up," Blaine said. When there was no reply he leaned over her and shook her by the shoulders. She wasn't wearing her seatbelt. "Bunny." With a certain amount of dread Blaine hitched up the skirt covering her injured leg. Ominously the wound had bled very little onto the bandages but the cloth was still slightly damp – the gash was weeping. "Fuck." Blaine ground his teeth and looked around the car park. It was 11:00am and the services were fairly busy, there was no way he could carry her out of the car.

"Bunny!" Blaine slapped her face and when she still didn't stir he pinched her injured thigh.

"Ah!" Bunny opened her eyes with a cry.

"You've gotta get up." Blaine was already opening his car door.

"No." Bunny's eyes were glazed and her head began to tilt back again.

"Yes." Blaine came around to the passenger side and cruelly pulled her out onto the tarmac. The pain that went through her when her feet touched the ground jolted her more awake with another cry.

"Where are we?" Bunny gasped.

"Services outside Heathrow. I need to get you into that hotel." Blaine pointed to the Travelodge. "Then you can sleep, okay?"

"I need to get –"

"Not now. Shut up and walk."

Dumbly Bunny nodded and accepted his proffered arm. With his support she managed a vaguely normal walk to the hotel lobby. Once they entered the cheap, heated building Blaine left her propped against the edge of the counter while he spoke to the receptionist. He was a young man with greasy yellow hair and a rumpled uniform.

"Hi," Blaine said. "I need a twin room for a night."

"I'm afraid we only have doubles left. Is that okay?"

Blaine briefly debated the merits of having two rooms but decided against it. "That'll be fine."

"Ensuite?"

"Yes please."

"And," Bunny spoke up suddenly from the corner, "can you send up some ice? I've twisted my angle."

The receptionist actually looked her up and down. He grinned. "No problem."

Bunny turned away and studied the pot plants.

Blaine fixed his eyes on the boy. "Are you quite done?"

"Sure." The receptionist looked down at his computer. "Sorry. I just need your card."

Blaine pushed over his Visa and was shortly repaid with a room key. Even though the room was only on the second floor they took the lift. Once they reached the right floor Bunny checked up and down the corridor and visibly sagged when there was no one in sight.

"Come on." Blaine half-carried her to their room and pushed the electronic key in with one hand. The door swung open, revealing a small dark space with a double bed and basic furniture. Bunny stumbled to the bed and eased herself onto it with a sigh, gently swinging her bad leg up onto the mattress.

She looked down at her leg then up at Blaine. "This is serious, isn't it?"

"Yeah."

"Fuck." Bunny sagged against the pillows and stared up at the ceiling. "I don't like it here."

"These hotels are always horrible."

"No, I mean away from Tokyo. It's all so beautiful there."

"Beautiful?"

"Sure. Don't you think so? All bright lights and rain and a million souls flickering in the darkness."

"You're delirious."

There was a smile in her green eyes. "I know."

"We need to do something about your leg."

"I think it's infected."

"I know it is. Look, I have this mate, a guy I knew back in the forces. He was a field doctor but when he came out he went a bit bent. You know? I think he's stopped all the underground stuff, I think he's straight now, but I reckon he still might do something outside the law if it's for me."

"You think I need more than a couple of penicillin, then?"

"Yeah."

"Okay. Call him. But it can't take long – I need to get to Pottersby. Tonight. If I don't Faber might guess…" The red spots were returning on her cheeks. "I'm going to end it." Her voice trailed off and her eyes closed again.

Blaine sat on the hard wooden chair and stared at Bunny for a while. Her hair was covered in dust and the horrible patterned skirt was too big for her.

There was a knock at the door and Blaine opened it to find a maid holding a bucket of ice. "Thank you," he said as he took it and shut the door with his foot.

He put the bucket down on the dresser and snapped open his phone, scrolling through the silver menus to find a number he hadn't called in over two years. The phone rang and rang and Blaine imagined Harry staring at it, deciding whether or not to pick up. Eventually he did.

"Harry Cooper."

"Hey, Harry, it's me."

A pause. "Major O'Dwyer! And what do you want, my favourite old sod?"

"A favour." Blaine grimaced into the receiver. "An off the record one."

"Blaine, you know I'm clean now. I'm a partner, got a wife and kid."

"I know. But I really, really need your help. As a doctor. Hippocratic oath and all that. I've got someone with me, they need help urgently but they can't go to a hospital, you know?"

Another pause. "How bad is it?"

"Bad. A big gash through her thigh. I tried to splint it but it's infected, she keeps going comatose on me."

"Ha! A she?" Harry's voice warmed up. "So this isn't some gang-related warfare thing you're dragging me into?"

"No! Not at all. There's a warrant out for her arrest but that's it Harry, I swear. And she's innocent for that anyway."

"Oh, all right then. You'll come to the surgery?"

"Uh… I don't think I can move her. Can you come here?"

"Where's here?"

"A Travelodge on the M25. It's the nearest one to Heathrow."

"Jesus, Blaine! Oh, all right. I'll come but it'll take me a few hours."

"Uh, it can't really wait a few hours."

Harry growled. "All right. But this had better be damn good."

"Thanks man, I owe you one."

"You owe me more than one." Harry hung up.

Blaine smiled to himself and set about unwrapping the bandages on Bunny's leg so he could pack some ice around the wound.

Harry was as good as his word and showed up at midday with a doctor's bag stashed under one arm. He was in his forties, a slightly fat man with a rounded smiley face and greying hair.

"So where is she?"

"Through here." Blaine clapped him on the back then stepped aside to let him into the room. He'd drawn the curtains and put all the table lamps on – the place didn't seem quite so dismal that way.

"Shit." Harry put his bag on the floor and knelt over the bed to get a look at Bunny's leg. It was a sign of his fascination for all things medical that he didn't so much as glance at her face. "This is bad."

The wound, now uncovered, looked much worse than it had in Tokyo. The fresh blood had been replaced by an angry red mess, the skin all around the weeping gash pink and puckered. "You did the first aid yourself? And the splint?"

"Yeah."

"Well," Harry frowned. "It's helped a bit. It needs a proper clean and stitches though. Why did you leave it so long before calling me?" Blaine opened his mouth to reply but the doctor ran straight over him. "No, wait, don't tell me. I don't wanna know. Come on, let's get started.

The next hour passed slowly. Harry painstakingly cleaned the wound, removed the remains of Blaine's glue and examined the flesh at length. He pulled out two tiny slivers of metal covered in gunk and dropped them into a tissue with a queer look at Blaine. He didn't ask what had caused the injury and Blaine didn't tell him. Eventually the doctor sewed the wound up again and gave Bunny a massive dose of penicillin. He re-splinted the leg using a hard plastic device from his bag and threw away the broken umbrella handle. When he was finished it was nearly 1:30pm.

"There, all over," Harry said with a tired grin.

"Thanks," Blaine stuck out his hand. "I'll buy you lunch."

"Nah, it's enough to know I helped a wanted criminal recover from a stab wound. I've gotta get back to work now or my wife'll find out and kill me."

"Well, then thanks again. I'll pay you back sometime."

"Maybe." Harry grinned again. "Kinda like the old days, huh?"

Blaine smiled, even though for him it felt nothing like the old days. "Yeah, buddy. See ya soon."

"Bye-bye." Harry turned and went out through the door, his bag tucked under his arm.

Blaine sat on the chair again, staring at the slow rise and fall of Bunny's chest. She'd remained unconscious throughout the entire procedure and Harry had said she'd sleep for at least another few hours. After a few minutes Blaine climbed into bed beside her, leaving Bunny to sleep on top of the covers while he crawled under them on the other side.

Blaine was awoken at 3:00pm by Bunny shaking his arm.

"Hey, wake up!" she said, smiling.

"Hey." Blaine sat up in bed and looked at her. Her eyes had lost that feverish glaze and her skin was a more normal colour. "How's the leg?"

"Much better." She pulled back the blanket the doctor had draped over her and showed him. The wound had healed an enormous amount – the skin was no longer puffy and the bandages were clean. "Thank you."

"You're welcome. Although it wasn't really me."

"Yeah, but it was your mate, and you looking after me. Thank you." Her eyes were fixed on him and Blaine felt momentarily caught.

He pulled himself out of bed, the thick hairs on his chest contrasting with the white sheets. He pulled his jeans on over his boxer shorts. "You'll need to rest it for a couple of days."

There was silence from the bed behind him. Blaine drew the curtains and tried not to turn around.

In a small, quiet voice Bunny said "I can't."

"Why?"

"I have to go now. I've been waiting for the past three months. And now Faber knows I was in Tokyo he might guess… It has to be now."

"I won't help you anymore unless you tell me what's going on. I need to understand."

A shaft of wintry afternoon sunlight hit Bunny's face and made her hair shine white. She spoke softly. "Yes, you will."

Blaine snapped around. "Why?"

"Why won't I tell you what's going on, or why will you help me even though I won't?"

"Both."

Bunny shrugged and in the movement Blaine detected something of the girl who had tackled him when he'd broken into her apartment. "I won't tell you what's going on because I don't trust you, even now. When I first met you Faber had hired you to kill me. If I tell you what I know how do I know you won't turn on me, tell him everything I've just said? Faber can pay you for your help. I can't."

Blaine's eyes flashed but he stayed silent.

"And," Bunny continued, "as to why you'll help me even if I don't… Well, I don't quite know for sure. A feeling, shall we say? A thrumming in my bones." She tilted her chin up at him, her green eyes unreadable. "I think you need this." Her voice became even softer. "I think you found something in that subway that you thought you'd lost. Some sort of quest for redemption? I think you've been lost for awhile, but now you've seen a way out of it." Her voice strengthened. "So yes, I think you'll continue to help me even though you don't know what's going on. If I'm wrong then you can leave, of course. I never expected help. I can do this on my own."

Blaine swallowed and sat down on the bed beside her. "You can't," he whispered. "Not when you're sick like this."

"I'm going, today, whether I'm sick or not. If you want to come then… your help would be appreciated. If not then that's fine too. You've paid for a night here; just stay and recover from your jetlag. It doesn't change anything."

"You know I'm going to come. But this…" Blaine's mind flicked back to Bunny melting through a wall, to the spoon hovering in the rubble. "Doesn't the stuff that's been happening screw with your head? Aren't you scared it'll drive you mad?"

Bunny smiled gently. "Why do you think I ended up high every night?"

She slid off the bed and went into the bathroom. After a minute Blaine started getting dressed.

At 3:30pm the pair checked out and then crossed the road into the dingy Little Chef for lunch. They both ordered Full English breakfasts and when it arrived Bunny ate like she'd never seen food before. Two sausages, eggs, bacon, black pudding and hash browns disappeared before Blaine's amazed eyes.

"Feeling better?" he asked, the first words he'd uttered since their confrontation in the bedroom.

"Sorry," Bunny replied, and blushed. It reminded Blaine that only three months ago she'd been a shy school teacher.

"So," he said once the plates were cleared away. "Where is it we need to go?"

"Pottersby. That's where Faber is."

"No, I saw Faber right before I left. He was in his London offices."

"Not any more he won't be."

"How do you know?"

She looked uncomfortable. "There really are things I don't wanna tell you."

"Okay, okay. Can you tell me anything? What are you going to do when we get there?"

"It's complicated." Bunny took another look at Blaine's face and remembered how he'd carried her into the hotel room. Perhaps she could trust him a bit? "Look, when Faber visited Tokyo he found something. Something very valuable. It's the source of his wealth – how he went from being a psychiatrist in a tiny office to owning a skyscraper. My father tried to take this thing away from him, expose Faber as a thief, and that's why Faber killed him. He wants to kill me because I know about it, I could expose him too. If people found out what he'd stolen… he'd lose everything. The money, the power, the prestige. Everything."

"But you don't wanna tell me what this thing is?"

"No. But I know that Faber's in Pottersby because that's where *it* is – he kept it at my father's house and if he thinks I might be coming to England he'll go back for it."

"Why didn't you try to stop Faber earlier? Why run to Japan?"

"Because I didn't know everything then! And because I wasn't thinking straight. My father had died. But now it's different. Look, you really don't have to come with me."

"You know I'm coming."

"I guess I do. And I'm grateful. But you should know, where we're going, my father's house… it's protected."

"Armed guards?"

Bunny shrugged. "Maybe. But I'm not really worried about that. I'm worried about the weird stuff."

"Like being attacked by pumpkins weird?"

"What?" Bunny looked genuinely bewildered.

"When I searched your flat in Lowestoft I was attacked by these flying Halloween pumpkins. I tried to convince myself it was just kids throwing them through the window but… it was bizarre."

A queer expression passed over Bunny's face. "Yeah. Stuff like that. But much worse, I think. I don't know for sure what'll be there - just that it'll be bad. It's Faber."

Blaine nodded and wordlessly finished his coffee.

Twenty minutes later they began the drive to Shropshire. Although the afternoon had promised weak sunshine it didn't hold for long and the November weather soon turned bleak as dark clouds filled the sky. They started driving just after 4:00pm and within an hour of cruising down the M40 Blaine switched the heating off. The humidity was just too high.

"So," Bunny said at one point. "Tell me how Faber hired you."

And so Blaine told the story – the strange letter he'd received, the meeting in Faber Enterprises and the scientist's bizarre insistence that Bunny was in Tokyo. After he'd finished Bunny sat quietly for a few moments, thinking. Eventually she began to quiz him about himself.

"So how did you become a private investigator?"

Blaine shrugged. "When I left the police it just seemed like the natural thing to do. As natural as when I came out of the Army and went into the force."

"You were in the Army? For how long?"

"Thirteen years. I joined when I was eighteen."

"What rank did you reach?"

Blaine remembered Harry calling him by his old title. "Major."

"Wow." Bunny paused again. "You must have killed a lot men. You saw action in the Balkans?"

"Yeah." Blaine said shortly.

After that they didn't talk for a while. Blaine put the stereo on and Radio 1 filled the car. Apparently the DJ liked dance music – hard bass blared out of the speakers. It wasn't that Blaine was angry with Bunny for asking the question – once you told people you'd served in the Army they sooner or later all asked it. How many men *had* he killed? He honestly didn't know. When he'd been in Yugoslavia he'd killed many – perhaps between twenty and forty people. It was hard to tell when you were using bombs or machine guns. He still remembered the smell of the earth and the way it had mixed with the blood and sweat of the men around you. He remembered the stench of fear and the intense pressure. He'd been sent in 1991 at the tender age of twenty-two and had learnt far too much too quickly – he'd been as young and impressionable as a block of wax. He didn't regret those years or the deaths he'd caused; he had believed in what he'd been doing. While in the police he'd killed two more men, both in self-defence while on active duty. He'd risen just as quickly through the blue ranks as he had through those of the green – it turned out he had a quick mind as well as quick reflexes. He'd loved the four years he'd spent in the force. His life had been good, he'd been happy with himself. But after that... everyone always asked the wrong question. It didn't matter how many men he'd killed. It was the number of *women* that mattered. And he'd only ever killed one.

Half an hour later Blaine could stand his private musings no longer so he rummaged in the hollow beneath the gear stick and handed Bunny his iPod.

"Pick something," he said.

"Thanks," said Bunny. She recognised that this was his way of apologising for being so short with her before – she'd obviously hit a nerve.

A few minutes later the sound of the *Smashing Pumpkins* pervaded the car and Blaine heard Bunny singing along to one of the songs:

'The useless drag of another day, the endless drags of a death rock boy

Mascara sure and lipstick lost, glitter burned by restless thoughts of being forgotten

And in your sad machines you'll forever stay.'

Her head was tilted back against the headrest and she was wearing a slight smile. Blaine noticed her fingers drumming on the dashboard. He wouldn't have imagined she'd like heavy rock after the stuff he'd seen her dancing to in Tokyo.

"'And in your sad machines you'll forever stay?'" Blaine asked, when the song had finished.

Bunny replied without opening her eyes. "One can only hope."

Although Blaine didn't understand her answer he let it go, content to have the car filled with strong drums and guitar. They drove on. After two hours he switched from the M40 to the A458 and signs for Shrewsbury started appearing.

"We're getting closer," he said, and Bunny nodded.

Blaine pushed the car to go even faster – hitting 80mph – and they roared on.

When they were past Shrewsbury Bunny asked Blaine to stop at another set of services on the A5. These services were bigger than the last and contained a Tesco. Bunny beckoned Blaine to it excitedly and once they were inside she took him over to the clothes section.

"I'm sick of wearing this gypsy skirt," she said as she pulled a pair of jeans from the racks.

"You think those will fit over the splint?"

"They will if I buy men's, they're wider in the leg." Bunny proceeded to pick out a clean t-shirt for herself and some underwear. "You sure you don't want anything? We've been wearing the same clothes for two days."

With a shrug Blaine bowed to her logic and bought some new clothes too, all on his credit card.

They changed in the supermarket toilets and in the mirror even Blaine had to admit the pale blue shirt made him look fresher. When he walked out of the men's toilets though and saw Bunny the improvement was much more drastic. The jeans suited her slim figure better than the tatty skirt ever had and the bulge of the splint wasn't too visible underneath the bulky fabric. The tight green t-shirt showed off her eyes and she'd combed her hair back into a ponytail. She looked prettier and younger.

"Whoops," she said, disregarding his stare. "Forgot the belt." She threaded the thick leather through the belt loops – it was not dissimilar to the one she'd worn in Tokyo – and Blaine blinked at the sudden sight of her pale, taut stomach when the trousers slipped off her hips.

"Come on," he said gruffly. He led them back to the car and they started driving again.

For the next quarter of an hour the air was thick but relaxed between them. Bunny munched on a chicken and mayo wrap and tried to concentrate on the music. She did not want to remember the last time she'd made this journey. Strangely the weather helped - soon after their Tesco stop at 6:00pm the rain started pelting down. It was a proper English thunderstorm, lightening flashed in the distance and the rain fell in great white sheets. The spray on the road was so thick it covered the surface in a heavy mist; Blaine could barely see five feet ahead of him and was forced to cut his speed in half. All around him other drivers were doing the same. The windscreen wipers were on full-pelt but they hardly made any difference.

Bunny paused the music and leaned forward to stare into the grey windscreen. "Shit," she murmured.

"We'll be okay, we're barely half an hour away now."

"I know," she said in a soft, distracted tone. "That's what's worrying me."

Blaine shot her a look, his dark eyebrows furrowed. "You're not thinking -"

"I don't know." Bunny stared at the water running in tiny torrents down the glass. "Maybe."

They drove on in silence, listening to the rain thunder on the soft-top roof. Bunny cracked her window open and breathed in the rain-smell. Another half hour passed and the traffic became slower and slower while night began to fall outside.

"Take the next exit," Bunny suddenly commanded.

"Is it the right one?"

"No, but it's better than nothing. If we keep going this slowly it'll be midnight before we reach Owestry."

Blaine nodded and moved into the left-hand lane, the radio now on low, and Bunny began to direct him through Knock and deep into the Shropshire countryside.

"You're looking for signs to Llwynmawr," she said at one point as they drove past yet another little town. "It's north of here, just over the English-Welsh border."

"I thought your father lived in Pottersby?"

"He does, I mean he did, but there'll be no signs for anywhere that small."

"How small is it?"

Bunny snorted. "Tiny. Population of under a hundred."

"That's not big enough for a village!"

"Ha! No, not nearly. Pottersby isn't even big enough to be a hamlet. It's just a collection of twenty or so houses in the middle of a valley."

Blaine shook his head. "I can't imagine living anywhere so small. I grew up in Dublin in a crowded city block."

Bunny looked at him, surprised. She studied his wide jaw, the stubble on his face that was threatening to turn into a beard, the muscles on his arms. His face was impassive, his eyes gave little away. The was the first time he'd volunteered anything about his personal life. She opened her mouth to ask him more but an emergency travel update interrupted her on the radio.

"We've just received news that the A5 is now at a total standstill, due to an overturned lorry that crashed through both lanes. We understand it hit two cars and a small van. It's unknown how many casualties there are but the accident is thought to have been caused by the heavy storms that started in Shropshire earlier this afternoon. Motorists are advised not to travel if at all possible, as visibility is now down to fifteen percent and the rain shows no sign of abating -" Bunny switched it off.

"He knows we're coming," she said quietly.

Blaine listened to the tapping of the rain on the roof. "You really think he's causing this? How?"

"The same way he caused the earthquakes. Look, it's okay if you don't believe me, I understand. If you stay with me it'll all become clear."

Blaine merely nodded and continued to drive into the rain.

Over the next half hour night fell completely outside and the rain increased in its ferocity. By 7:00pm Blaine had his fog lights on full beam and was crawling along the narrow country roads at 15mph. They'd passed Llwynmawr some time ago and he was now relying totally on Bunny's mental map of the area to get them where they needed to go. They hardly passed any cars and the lanes they travelled through gradually got smaller and bumpier until it seemed to Blaine that they were only fit for tractors. After an eternity of dark hedgerows and deep puddles that splashed mud up the sides of the car Bunny clapped her hands excitedly. "We're here."

Blaine stared out through the black windscreen but couldn't see a thing past the hedges that rose up on either side of the hill he was on. "Where?"

"Just go forward a few more yards and switch off your headlights… there!"

And then Blaine saw Pottersby. His car breasted the hill and he gently brought it to a stop as he looked down on the distant cluster of glittering lights. The night was too dark for him to make out anything in detail; the valley stretched out perhaps half a mile below them and the hills on the far side were covered in trees. To his left lay a cornfield and to his right an orchard of bare, low-sitting apple trees. The only lights came from the small collection of houses nestled at the foot of the valley; it was like looking down at a group of candles on the far side of a garden.

Bunny wound her window down, oblivious to the rain, and pointed to the left of the lights. "My father's house is actually in Bayleir Forest, behind Pottersby."

"How do we get there?" Blaine half-shouted over the rain.

Bunny wound the window back up. "Normally I'd drive through the valley and then walk the last little bit through the trees, but I don't wanna go past the houses tonight. Faber would know."

"What then?"

"Turn left, into that field. We can -"

"This car isn't a 4x4!"

"I know. But if we drive through the field we can hide it behind some trees, then hike the rest of the way."

Involuntarily Blaine looked down at Bunny's leg. "Are you sure?"

"Do you have a better idea?"

Blaine ground his teeth. "You planned this! You knew if you told me in advance there's no way I'd let you do it. You'll cripple yourself!" He thumped his palms on the steering wheel and glared at her. Although the headlights were off the neon rings around the clock and speedometer glowed green and her elfin face was gifted with eerie shadows.

Bunny tossed her hair. "You can still leave. Let me get out, you turn around and drive back. Find an inn or something."

Blaine growled. "No." With a violent jerk of the wheel he turned the car into the field and tried to navigate through the plants. Bunny said nothing as he slowly manoeuvred the car onto the flattest part of the ground by the hedge and she stayed silent until they reached the far edge of the field.

"There," she murmured as a line of trees came into sight. "There's a hollow on the far side of those ones on the right, you can leave it there and pick it up after."

Blaine nodded wordlessly as he parked it, just on the edge of the road. As awkward as the manoeuvre was it was also clever – no one would find the car here. As he pulled up the handbrake he noticed that the rain had begun to slacken.

"You see?" Bunny said. "It'll be fine after all. Now we walk."

Blaine nodded and got out of the car. His trainers sank into the soft earth but there was too much undergrowth for it to be really muddy. He walked around to the back of the car and took out the gun he'd stashed there before his trip to Japan, tucking it into the waistband of his trousers. Somewhere far away two fireworks shot up into the sky and exploded in a shiver of silver sparks.

"Do you only have one gun?" Bunny's pupils were wide.

Blaine considered lying but didn't. "No." He pulled his last piece out of the boot and threw it to her.

"Thanks." Bunny tucked it into her belt and pushed a stray lock of hair away from her face. She looked like some sort of screwed-up cowgirl in the jeans and hiking boots she'd bought for herself. The rain was slowing but had already begun to soak the cotton of her t-shirt.

"You didn't think to buy a coat on your shopping trip?" Blaine asked, already pulling his heavy winter jacket out of the back of the car.

"No." Her teeth flashed white as she grinned. "Why, you have a spare?"

Blaine laughed. "Kinda." He chucked her his rain poncho – it was still far too big but at least it was dry. "You'll have to roll the sleeves up."

"No worries." Bunny unfolded the yellow plastic and began wadding up the excess fabric. Once she was done she pointed a finger into the darkness of the trees beside them. "Faber's somewhere in there."

"Bunny?"

"Yeah?"

"You really think he sent the storm?"

There was a flash of yellow as the hood of the poncho tilted to one side ahead of him. She'd already begun walking. "Yeah. I really do. And I *really* think he knows we're coming."

"Why are you so sure?" Blaine asked as he followed her carefully through the thick trees and dense undergrowth. He couldn't see more than a foot in front of his face and the ground was slippery with rain. He could still hear water pelting down onto the leaves above but mercifully little of it made it to ground level. He followed the quick canary ahead of him, amazed she seemed to know her way so well through the dark forest. Suddenly Bunny came to a halt in front of him and she grabbed his arm.

"Because of that," she whispered, pointing at something between the trees up ahead.

Blaine strained his eyes and at first he could make out nothing beyond the silhouette of some trees. Then he realised that the only reason he could make out a silhouette at all was because of the luminous green mist rising behind them.

CHAPTER 10

The mind shifted in its green seabed, moving around dim lights and sunken buildings. It drifted through ocean chasms and sees a little boy, far away at the bottom of a well...

The boy is trying on the head machine again, its silver contours freshly reworked. He sinks into it, feels the changes occur, and this time is directed towards a new world of stocks and shares and math. He moves little bits inside the computers, gets inside the binary codes, sees where this integer has to go, and this one, and that.

What he needs to do doesn't take long but every day he is pushed to do more and more and the head machine improves and improves, until one day...

* * *

Blaine stared at the mist, involuntarily moving closer to Bunny in his terror. "What the hell is that?"

Bunny took a tighter grip on the butt of her gun. "I have no idea." She shifted her body so that Blaine could walk next to her. "Let's find out."

Warily the two approached, picking their way around trees and over low shrubs and ancient fallen branches. The air was black and still; the rain could still be heard pattering onto leaves somewhere high above but it no longer fell at all to the forest floor. Somewhere in the distance an owl hooted but was suddenly cut off. Miles away another firework went off but this time Blaine couldn't see its sparks.

He watched the green mist dance up ahead and realised that a hush had fallen over the wood. It was not unlike the quiet he'd experienced following Kazuto through the greenly shadowed alleys of Tokyo. He wanted to speak, to break the spell, but the words stayed locked in his mouth. They approached slowly and as they got closer Blaine was able to make out more of the mist. He realised it wasn't really a mist at all, more like a thick green-grey coloured smoke that contained dancing glittery pinpricks of light. When they were a few yards away they both stopped, hypnotised by the way the lights danced off the mossy trunks and bounced off the muddy ground. Bunny slipped her hand into Blaine's – the soft, unexpected touch sent a thrill through him – and she gently tugged him around to start walking back to the car. Blaine followed her happily, as docile as a lamb. A few tendrils of mist wrapped around their feet and picked their way for them, even though their eyes stared blankly into darkness.

When they were nearly at the car Bunny shrieked. "No!"

Blaine blinked, still feeling stupid, and felt her hand wrench out of his as she twisted away to run back towards the misty copse.

"I won't let you!" Bunny cried, stumbling as she sprinted towards the smoke, both arms stretched out in front of her.

Blaine stood still, feeling warm and drowsy. It was only when he saw Bunny stumble headfirst into the cloying stuff that the dumbness began to recede and his head cleared.

"Stop!" he tried to call, although his lips shaped only 'Sh'.

Blaine forced himself to move and ran forward to see Bunny disappear beneath the mist. She seemed to have fallen to the ground, was sitting with her legs stretched out in front of her and her face tilted upwards. The smoke enveloped her body completely – Blaine could see only the tip of one of her boots poking through – and tendrils of it were curling up around her face and neck. Her mouth was wide open, as if she were trying to catch raindrops, and little glittery particles danced on her tongue. Blaine yelled and continued full-pelt into the smoke. Instantly he was blinded. His eyes saw nothing but greyness and his reaching hands brushed only trees.

"Bunny!" He tried to shout but any sound that emerged was muffled instantly.

Blaine stood still and tried to get his bearings. He had faced worse than this before. He blinked and willed his eyes to start working. Eventually he began to see more than the grey-green shapes that moved in the corners of his vision – he started to see sparks shooting through the murk. As he stood still he began to make out more details in the green; he thought he saw the silhouettes of people and once a dragon. He began to feel warm and peaceful. He watched - confused but placid - as a white dragon drifted past him with its jaws open. He thought he saw steam coming out of its mouth.

Suddenly a hand gripped Blaine's right leg and he was pulled down out of his reverie.

"Blaine!" Bunny was shouting at him, had been for some time.

Blaine hunkered down on the floor beside her, her face emerging like a fairy's out of the mist. "What's going on?" He felt as if he were dreaming.

Bunny looked drawn and worried. "This is… a friendly warning. Not to go any further. He can't stop us, not really, but he's trying."

"Faber?"

"No. Not Faber." She looked around, her expression haunted. "I wish my father was here."

"Bunny." Blaine grabbed her chin and turned her face back towards him. The mist grew thicker for a moment, a sheet of it blowing past her face and obscuring it. "What do we need to do?"

"Go through the forest." She cocked her head to one side. "But it'll be bad, really bad, in there. Faber has control over it now."

"Over what?"

"All of it. All of Bayleir Forest. And we don't have much time. Once he knows we're this close he might act on what he guesses and if he suspects the extent of what's been going on he'll do something terrible."

Blaine leaned his stubbly face close to Bunny's, to see her better in the smoke. Her green eyes glowed luminously in the dark. "What will he do?"

"He'll kill someone else I care about."

Uncomprehending, but recognising the urgency in Bunny's eyes, Blaine pulled her up off the forest floor and set her grimly on her feet.

"Which way?"

Bunny pointed deeper into the forest. "Down there."

The pair walked on determinedly, the mist growing thicker around them and the glitter more agitated. Bunny had been right though – it couldn't actually stop them. There were times that even though Blaine was touching Bunny's shoulder he couldn't see her in front of him; the mist grew greener and darker the deeper they went. A noise started to echo in his ears – a kind of wailing – and the mist before them grew almost black. Just as Blaine was about to halt and take stock of his surroundings it stopped. Like magic, the black smoke cleared and the ringing in his ears subsided.

"We're on our own now," Bunny murmured.

Blaine didn't reply, he was too busy taking in the beautiful scene in front of him. A winter wonderland stood before them. A large, roughly oval forest pool sat before them, surrounded by tall oaks and weeping willows whose branches draped over the lake. The water was completely iced over and the silvery surface gleamed as if it was lit from within. The tree branches were laden with snow even though they hadn't all lost their leaves and they obscured the night sky overhead. The snow glittered and glassy icicles hung from the branches, winking in the dark. Blaine took another step forward and his boot crunched on frosty undergrowth.

"Where now?" he whispered.

Bunny's face was pale. "Around to the right. But this cold isn't natural. I don't like it."

Blaine nodded and began to move around the right shore of the lake, trying to be quiet. There was no sound here other than that created by their passing; they couldn't hear any more birds. It was glacially cold, Blaine felt himself starting to shiver and pulled his coat tighter. Their footsteps crunched in slow unison and he heard Bunny breathing in front of him. His own breath was coming in great huffs of steam. The lake seemed larger than he'd first realised – it was taking an eternity to move around it.

They had been walking for just over five minutes when Blaine saw the first *thing*. Out of the corner of his left eye, just as he was moving beneath a heavily snow-laden branch, he saw a black shape move on the far side of the ice. It looked formless, like a billowing grey shadow.

Blaine stopped and pointed. "Did you see that?"

"What?"

"Never mind. Maybe I imagined it."

They continued on for another few minutes and then Bunny gave a quickly muffled shriek. "Look!" She pointed to the right, into the forest.

Another of the shapes was floating between the trees, it looked like some sort of dark wraith. It had vague arm shapes but no face or legs, it was totally black except for the edges that faded to grey. One of its 'arms', that was really little more than a tubular tendril, brushed the trees as it passed. Where the arm touched the frosty barks they turned black and disintegrated. The trees were left with dusty black holes gouged into their sides.

"Jesus Christ," whispered Blaine. And then: "There's another one!" He pointed straight ahead of him, to the edge of the lake they were traversing, and this time the wraith seemed to turn from side to side as if sniffing out a scent. Bunny grabbed Blaine's arm but otherwise stood still, her fingernails digging into the fabric of his jacket. The two of them stood motionless, trying to avoid becoming prey. But it was too late. The wraith in front of them made a high keening noise and swung around to face them. The one in the trees behind them followed suit and suddenly both grey shapes were moving towards them at vicious speed, leaving blackened dead undergrowth in their wake.

"Run!" Bunny grabbed Blaine's arm and turned to go back the way she'd come but a third formless thing had moved into the path.

"Here!" Blaine shouted and wrenched her back by the elbow, pulling her onto the icy surface of the lake.

He almost slid when his feet hit it but thankfully there was enough of a light dusting of snow on the surface for his trainers to get a grip. He didn't stop to worry that the ice might not take their weight – he was too worried about the evil things behind them that could melt his limbs to black dust if they touched him. The pair sprinted out over the ice, Bunny's hair streaming out golden behind them. They ran on and on not looking back, hearing the wails of the frustrated creatures in their ears. When Blaine did risk a look around he saw that eight or nine of them were in hot pursuit. He followed the curve of the lake round in a rough semi-circle and as they rounded the corner he pulled Bunny off the main pool onto a narrow ribbon of ice that led deeper into the forest. As soon as they embarked on the frozen stream it got darker, the trees thicker and the shadows deeper. But as they stumbled along the silver band the wails of the creatures seemed further away, until eventually they could only be heard at some distance behind them.

"Blaine," Bunny whispered when their pace began to slow. "We have to get off the stream. They'll track it. We have to hide."

Blaine didn't bother to reply, just pulled her off the frozen rivulet into the undergrowth. He pushed his way through thick trees and icy branches, his legs often sinking unto his knees in foliage.

"There," Bunny pointed.

Blaine followed her finger towards an old oak, its roots huge and full of shadowy hollows. He made his way towards it and sank into the deepest hollow, an arch made up of three huge twisting roots. It was full of moss. There was easily room for both of them and after settling his body inside, satisfied that they weren't visible from outside the tree, he beckoned Bunny in after him. She crawled inside and settled herself between his legs with her back against his stomach, her head tilted back against his chest.

"You think we're safe here?" Blaine asked. He was uncomfortably aware of her warmth between his thighs.

"I think so. The wraiths will figure out we escaped onto the stream, and they'll probably follow it for awhile, but they'll have no idea where in the forest we are so hopefully if we stay put for a bit they'll lose our trail and start to spread out again."

"Have you seen those things before?"

Since Bunny wasn't facing him he couldn't see her face but Blaine felt her back muscles tense. "Yeah."

"In Japan?"

"No." She half turned her head to look at something in the forest and in profile Blaine saw what might have been tears glistening in her eyes.

"When?" he asked gently.

"The day I found my father's body."

"Ah." Blaine murmured. He put his arms around Bunny and hugged her tight against him. To his surprise she sank back against his chest. He was much taller than her and she tucked her head underneath his chin. He found himself stroking her hair, working it out of its high ponytail and smoothing it flat against her skull. "What happened?"

"He sent me a letter, to my flat in Lowestoft. There was a whole parcel of stuff but I didn't read any of it properly then. I just read the letter and did exactly what he told me not to do."

"What did it say?"

Wordlessly, Bunny pulled her fake passport out of her jeans. From the back page she took out a thin, much-folded piece of paper. She sat up and handed it to Blaine, who strained to read it in the faint light.

My darling daughter,

I have done a terrible thing. Six months ago I was approached by a seemingly benevolent man named Gideon Faber, who required my philosophical expertise on a psychiatric case. I gladly leant him my help and, I confess, continued to do so even when the project took a more sinister turn. Although I have gone this far I will go no further. I enclose details of the project, my own notes and his, in case my plans to stop it are thwarted. By the time you receive this letter I hope I will have sorted the whole mess out and this will only seem to be the ramblings of a foolish old man.

But, just in case, I ask you with much love to leave the country. Go anywhere you choose but get yourself out of the range of Faber's influence. He has become a rich and powerful man. I worry that you might be used against me, and now you have the files you are a threat to him.

Please, my beloved daughter, do not stop to question me. Just drive to an airport and wait for me to email you. Do not, under any circumstances, come to Pottersby.

Love always,

Robert.

Bunny remained motionless while Blaine read it, staring out into the forest.

Eventually Blaine spoke. "So what did you do?"

"What do you think I did?"

"You went straight to Pottersby."

"Yeah. Where I found his body swinging from a beam in the shrine outside his house."

"I'm so sorry."

"So am I." Bunny was silent for awhile. Somewhere above them it started raining again with a gentle pitter-patter on the leaves.

"So when did you see the wraiths?"

"After I found him. A statue in the shrine started to move and when I turned around there was this dark *thing* hanging in the doorway, in broad daylight. It was looking at me. I screamed out but there was nowhere to go. It brushed part of the plaster and it cracked and fell off. I knew it meant to kill me. I tried to run away but the only way out was through it, and then the statue flew off the alcove and into it and even though it crumbled to dust the wraith turned and I ran, I ran and ran, back through the woods and into my car. And as I did... something reached out to me."

"Bunny -"

"I can't tell you any more. Please don't ask me to. I can't betray him." She spoke quickly, her limbs tense. "After I escaped in my car I got some money then drove straight to Heathrow."

"What did you do with the parcel?"

"It's still in a safety deposit box at the airport. Any more questions? I think you know all the rest."

"Not quite!"

"Well, no." Bunny turned to him in the dark. He could just make out her narrow chin and her wide eyes. She was smiling queerly. "Not quite."

Blaine touched her cheek with a finger, tracing the line of her jaw. "Shush."

Bunny stared up at him and shifted slightly between his legs. Blaine was suddenly extremely aware of the weight of her crushed against his thighs, of the way she was trembling.

"You're cold," he said and slid the wet poncho over her head.

She raised her arms to help him and he caught another flash of her pale stomach. He caught a glimpse of the lacy fabric of her bra, plastered to her t-shirt through the rain. Slowly he took off his winter coat and began to drape it around her shoulders.

"How long do you think we should stay here?" he asked.

Bunny took a long time to answer, a strange look in her eyes. Her mouth was slightly open and Blaine could see the tips of her teeth. Perhaps it was just the adrenalin but he felt as if the air was charged between them.

"A short while," she whispered eventually. She slid the coat off her shoulders and put it onto the ground behind Blaine. She sat between his legs, trembling in a different way, and looked up at him with a nameless expression on her face.

She wouldn't ask, Blaine realised, and softly he stroked the curve of her cheek. Her green eyes shone dark and fey, her breath coming quicker. She seemed to be getting hotter against him and Blaine realised with a shock that he was already hard. He wanted her badly, he could see her nipples poking through the top and knew it wasn't due to the cold. She tilted her head against the palm of his hand and he stroked his thumb across her lips. His blue eyes were intense, almost fierce, when he leaned in to kiss her. The first touch of her lips was electric. He held the moment for a few seconds, his mouth barely touching hers, and felt her breath against his face. He licked her bottom lip, tasting her, and felt her shudder slightly. He took his time, moving his hands through her hair and pulling her closer against him. When his tongue ceased exploring and moved its way into her mouth Bunny actually gasped and her control seemed to snap. She kissed him wildly, pushing him back into the hollow of the tree and clawing at the buttons of his shirt. She'd ripped off two of them and managed to straddle him before Blaine recovered from the onslaught and with one hand pushed her prone to the ground. In the depths of the tree the roots were too low for him to sit up over her so he stretched himself flat on the ground beside her, keeping one hand on her chest to hold her down. He was much, much stronger than her.

"Shush," he whispered again, lying beside her and propped up on his spare elbow. Catlike, Bunny struggled under his weight and tried to claw at his buttons again but he began to slowly kiss her nose, her ears, the side of her lips and gradually she grew still. As he moved his mouth down the curve of her neck he felt her relax under him and gently he moved the hand that had been pinning her down so he could pull her t-shirt over her head. The black, lacy bra she'd bought earlier looked stunning against her creamy skin and Blaine held eye contact with her as he unbuttoned the rest of his shirt. He was a broad-shouldered, well-built man and Bunny's eyes tracked the bulge of his arm muscles to the thick hair on his chest to the more lightly furred stomach. She reached for the belt on his jeans but Blaine grabbed her tiny hands in one of his own and pinned her back down again. He gently slid her bra off and began kissing the hollow of her neck, his stubble scratching her as he moved down to kiss her nipples. She had slightly small but well-rounded breasts, the small nipples very hard and pink. When he took one into his mouth for the first time her whole back arched and she mewed like a kitten, wrapping her legs around his and tangling them closer. With his spare hand Blaine began to undo her belt and slid his finger down her warm stomach into her jeans. He drew a finger along the hem of her black pants and her hips arched up to meet him. He kept her left nipple in his mouth as he moved his hand down towards the hot, smooth centre of her.

She was already slick and when he began to stroke her softly she began to moan gently, her hands relaxing above her head. Blaine felt himself getting harder as he pleasured her and he was almost relieved when she whispered his name and moved her hands towards his belt again. This time he helped her, taking their shoes off before easing the jeans down over his hardness. They ended up taking off their own clothes because it was quicker and somewhere far away the rain began falling more heavily. Bunny went wild again when she finally saw him naked, tracing the straight lines of his hips down to his cock. She pulled him towards her and began kissing him fiercely but Blaine pushed her back onto the coat and held her with his left hand on her chest while he gently moved his right hand between her legs. She moaned and bucked under him, her hands clawing at him as she tried to pull him closer, but it was only when her moans became really desperate that he lay himself flat on top of her. Outside the hollow of their tree thunder began to growl and raindrops splashed down onto their exposed feet. Blaine lay with the tip of his cock just touching the wet opening to her and she quietened enough to look up into his eyes. Her injured leg was canted slightly off to one side and he could feel her nipples pressing into his chest. They stared into each others' eyes and Blaine realised that he was holding her hands flat by their sides.

"I want you," she murmured, eyes dark with the need.

"I know," he said and slid himself into her with one long deep thrust.

Bunny cried out at the pleasure and the small frisson of pain, then lost it totally as he began to move inside her. She let go of his hands and pulled her fingers through his hair, scratching down his back and pulling him in tighter and tighter until Blaine lost it too and the pair of them clawed at each other in the darkness, fucking desperately with their eyes tight shut, mouths searching and bodies pushing. Bunny remembered little of the detail afterwards - it was all blur of heat and skin – but she did remember bending like a bow under him when her first orgasm rushed through her like a wave of fire. Everything was blurred and tingling and when Blaine finally came inside her they collapsed in a sweaty, trembling embrace. Although neither noticed until much later, both of their legs had been splashed with mud as the rain had thundered down outside their hollow.

Blaine became aware of himself perhaps after twenty minutes of lying there exhausted underneath the tree, hearing the water run off the leaves and feeling Bunny's smooth nakedness beside him.

"Bunny," he murmured, stroking her hair where it lay fanned out over his chest. She didn't reply and he gave her a few more minutes while he let his heart rate slow back to normal. He hadn't had sex like that since… well, since three years ago. He pushed all thoughts of Lilly away.

"Wake up," he said again and shook Bunny a little harder this time. "We've been here for nearly two hours."

Bunny stirred and gradually opened her eyes. "Okay," she said. "We've gotta go." All business-like she began pulling on her clothes and she handed Blaine his shirt.

"You okay?" he asked.

"Yeah." She was pulling her t-shirt on over her head as she replied. As the cotton slid past her face she turned to look over at him over her shoulder with a tender smile. "Great, in many ways. But now we have to go."

Blaine nodded. He liked such pragmatism. The rain was falling all around them and he tried to dry his wet feet on his coat before putting his socks and shoes back on. "You think we lost the wraiths?"

"Yeah. I think we'd know if we hadn't."

"Do you know how to get to the house from here?"

"Sure. I grew up in these woods! I know them like the back of my hand."

Blaine nodded and held out his heavy coat. "You want this?"

Bunny smiled. "No, thanks. It's too big and at least with this one I can roll the sleeves up."

"Cool." Blaine finished dressing and stood up from underneath the shelter of their tree. Instantly his hair and coat became splattered with rain. "At least it's not snowing anymore."

Bunny laughed. "No! But that just makes me worry what else Faber will be cooking up. C'mon, this way." She led them off confidently into the forest.

The hike took nearly two hours through the dark trees and increasingly stormy weather; several times they caught glimpses of the black wraiths but they were always far away and easy to hide from. Bayleir Forest was beautiful, the leaves were all shades of golds and greens and the rain made everything glisten. As they trekked on the sounds of animals returned – they heard owls and the flapping of bats – and once Bunny thought she spied a fox.

Eventually she put out a hand, stopping them both in what seemed to Blaine to be a piece of forest no different to any other.

"The cottage is nearby."

Secretly Blaine was relieved – Bunny had started to limp over the last hour and although he had no doubt she'd put up with as much pain as necessary he knew that if she opened her stitches or broke the splint there would come a point where she simply could not walk.

"Where, exactly?" he asked.

"Well, the track that most people would approach the cottage from is to the south of it, the nearest place you can get to it by car is the shrine about half a mile away. But we've come up around it from the north-west. I know you can't see it but the house is actually just down that ridge."

"What do you want to do?"

"I want to know who's there before we go in. If it's just Faber... then at least we know we'll be greeted by more of the same. More of the wraiths and whatever other shit he's managed to conjure up. If there are armed guards in there as well..." Bunny shrugged. "Well, I'd rather know. I wanna go around to the south-west side, there's a little ditch I know we can hide in, and watch the house for a bit."

"And if there are armed guards?"

Bunny looked up at him. "I don't know. But this ends tonight."

Blaine sighed. "Okay. Lead on."

He followed her around some more trees and was slightly amazed when the roof of a cottage rose up ahead of them. The girl's sense of direction was so good she could have been in the army. They crept around the trees and tall bushes until Bunny found the ditch she'd promised.

"Get down," she said. "I just wanna wait here twenty minutes or so. See if we can see anything."

Blaine nodded and hunkered down beside her. Waiting was something he was well used to.

After a few minutes he realised that Bunny kept darting looks at him while watching the cottage.

"What is it?" Blaine asked.

"Can I ask you something?"

"Sure."

"Look, I don't mean to pry. But... now I feel I can. I wanted to ask you before. About what you said in Tokyo, in the subway tunnel... Look, you said you were in the police. How did you end up working for Faber?"

"I'm a PI. He hired me to find you."

"You know what I mean."

"Yeah. I do." Blaine sighed and scrubbed his hand across his face. "The truth is, it's complicated. Everything after being in the Army is complicated. You go from being told when you can eat, sleep and shit to having this total freedom."

"And that drove you to become an assassin?"

"No. I told you that I became a policeman after I left the Army. Well, I did. I rose to the rank of Inspector. I was *good* at it. Did it for four years. But being a policeman lacked… a certain something. Action, maybe. I'd been in the Balkans. And I was looking for something, I was too free to do anything I wanted, and one day something I wanted and shouldn't have done came along."

"What?"

Blaine flashed a glance at Bunny, but her eyes were fixed on the cottage below them. "Not what. Who."

Then she did turn to look at him. She'd always been quick. "Some*one* you shouldn't have done?"

"Yeah." *O Lilly, with your dark hair and killer nails.* "A suspect on a case. A big case. Three murders that looked connected, but maybe not. This woman," - *this bitch* - "knew all the victims. But so did a lot of people. And these murders, they were messy jobs. Knives. Lots of blood. Not really a woman thing, you know? When women kill they prefer to be far away, detached. Poison or guns. It's not just a cliché."

"And you slept with her."

Blaine laughed harshly. "Better than that. I fell in love with her." Rain ran down his neck.

A pause. "And it was her, who'd killed those people?"

"Yeah. I had no idea, until I slept with her for the first time. It was…" Blaine swallowed, not wishing to offend his most recent conquest. "I'm no green virgin, honey. It was something else. She was intense. But afterwards it turned out she had this whole preying mantis thing going on. Mate and then kill afterwards. I know that most psychopaths have a sexual angle, but even so. I was lucky to get out alive and I'm a military man. Those other poor sods didn't stand a chance."

Bunny digested this silently, trying to ignore his use of the pet-name 'honey' and the strange feeling it evoked in her chest.

"But why…" she said eventually. "I still don't understand. Why did you leave the police? How did you end up with Faber?"

Blaine sighed. "Have you ever killed a man?"

"No."

"Well, I have." Even though Blaine had given up smoking years ago he found himself dying for a cigarette. "I've killed lots. God knows how many in the war and two men while I was in the police. It's a horrible thing, and probably the most horrible thing about it is it that it gets easier every time. But I've never, ever, killed a woman. Where I grew up…" - *even on that dingy council estate he couldn't wait to escape from* - "there were rules, codes of conduct. Boys didn't hit girls. If a boy beat up a girl, even his girlfriend, it was awful, taboo, you know? It's the way I was raised. So when I had to kill this woman, this *bitch*," Blaine spat the word and tried not to remember the blood that had stained the linoleum of the kitchen floor, "it fucked me up. Big time. Oh sure, the case was closed. I was a hero to the regular coppers. But not to the older ones, the officers who guessed what had really happened. So I retired, set up O'Dwyer Investigations. But when Faber approached me asking if I'd kill another murderess for money I thought, why not? It might help make up for what happened with Lilly."

This was the longest speech Bunny had ever heard Blaine make and she listened to it with a growing sense of fear. She'd just given her body to this man and he was a killer… she'd only met him because he'd been hired to kill her. What the hell was she doing? She was going mad! Perhaps the drugs in Tokyo were taking their toll.

"Bunny," Blaine said softly. "Look at me."

Scared, Bunny turned her head towards him. The whites of her eyes were very visible.

"I'm telling you this so that you know me. I'm not a good man. I might be strong and brave but that doesn't mean anything, I'm lost right now. I've fallen down the rabbit hold and I don't have a hope in hell of understanding the crazy shit that's going on around you. But whatever is going on I understand that it's not right, that it's unnatural. You've told me that Faber is evil and I believe you. I want to help."

Bunny nodded slowly. "Okay."

"Now it's your turn. You tell *me* what's going on."

Bunny sighed. "Okay." She looked drawn and pale, her voice was very soft. "It's hard to explain. I don't understand all of it myself – perhaps only my father did. I'll tell you… what I can."

"Okay."

"It started in Tokyo, in the city." Bunny's voice became dreamy. "It all started there. I told you before that Faber discovered something. Something he'd never imagined could be real, something special. He did everything he could to get hold of it, trap it."

"What was he doing in Tokyo? What did he find?"

Bunny looked pained. "What he was doing there is easy: he's a psychiatrist. He was there for a conference. What he found is harder to describe, and at first even he didn't know what it was. It was after doing a lot of research that he contacted my father."

"How did they know each other?"

"I don't think they did, except through reputation. My father was a great figure in Philosophy of Mind. He was famous for his views on certain things. Anyway, Faber took this thing back to England and then he tried to make it do all the wonderful things he thought it should be able to."

"But it didn't?"

"No, it did. That's how Faber got so rich. But then he broke it. And that was when my father threatened to expose him - that was when all hell broke loose and my father died."

"What was it Faber found?"

Bunny opened her mouth to reply when suddenly the front door opened. "Look!" she whispered, jabbing Blaine in the ribs.

The pair of them stared at the cottage as yellow light spilled from the front door and an old man in a wheelchair came out of it. He opened his arms wide and cackled insanely out into the night. "I know you're there my little bunny, come out come out wherever you are!"

CHAPTER 11

The mind hung suspended in the liquid space, indigo ripples shooting through the green. The creature was scared, uncertain, the city streets picked out in emerald and vibrating. It sensed the motions - so far away - that the girl and her Irish gunman were making but it could do little... it was hidden here in this watery dark.

At some point during the violence the creature was pulled slowly into vortex, the ocean tides tugging this way and then that, dragging it down into memory.

It saw the white-haired man, tall and blue-eyed, enter the room and it felt his scrutiny. Heard the quick, angry words followed by compassionate demands. And then motion, a swaying bumpy ride through a building and into a car and then... and then into a blessed cool breeze. A forest, green shadows dancing on the leaves. And later a cool room with wide windows that touched the trees outside. Relief and light and dark. All distant and dim, seen from a distance. The white-haired man visited him often, the other less so. And then, one hot summer night, the white-haired one exploded in a fit of anger and righteousness so sudden it threatened to topple its captor.

And then it saw the blade, saw the flashing curving knife, saw the crimson blood spurt and felt the white-haired man fighting for his life. The memory faded here but the mind had known what to do. In its green amber there was no uncertainty. Later, there was movement while the police were called, but then even that was over too. The creature returned to its place amongst the green shadows.

* * *

Blaine and Bunny watched with wide eyes as the old man cackled. His wheelchair was held by the bulky Eluf and the bodyguard's large frame almost entirely blocked the light spilling from the front door so that the chair's occupant was obscured in shadow.

"Is that really Faber?" Blaine whispered.

"Yeah. I don't know who the big guy is, though."

"His name is Eluf Sondem. I met him at Faber Enterprises. A lovely man. He's definitely armed. Do you think Faber would have more guards?"

Bunny bit her lip. "Maybe. I don't know. No, actually, I think he'd be replying on more stuff like the wraiths."

"What *are* they?"

"I'm not quite sure. I just know they're on his side."

"Do you know any way we could get inside unnoticed? How are you planning on killing him?" Blaine touched the butt of his gun. "Maybe I could slide in through a window or something."

"No. It's too risky. He's got a hostage in there, a little boy."

"B-"

"Look, I mean it. Don't ask. Just trust me, okay? We need to get in and find him. Then we can kill Faber."

"Any bright ideas on how to do that? We can't just sneak into the cottage and look for him – the place looks tiny."

Bunny's shoulders sagged. "I guess I didn't think this through."

"All right." Blaine ran a hand through his hair. "Look, we've gotta split them up. How about I create some sort of diversion out here, try to lure at least one of them outside, and you sneak inside and look for the kid?"

"But what if they don't want to split up?"

"Why wouldn't they? As far as they're concerned the only person coming for them is you. They don't need to worry about not guarding their flank if they think you're making a lone frontal attack."

"Okay. All right, let's do it. What are you gonna do?"

"I'll think of something. You go round the side, see if you can get in through a window."

"Okay." Bunny pushed back the hood of her poncho. The rain had stopped but the air still felt heavy with moisture. "Thanks, Blaine. Really." She wanted to add something about the story he'd just gifted her with but couldn't find the words. "Thanks."

"You're welcome." Blaine's expression was unreadable as he watched her slither away through the undergrowth. Now he just needed to have a bright idea for the diversion.

Fifteen minutes later a large crash echoed through the forest and Eluf looked up from his seat by the fire. Gideon was half-sitting, half-lying in an alcove in the corner of the room that led on to the kitchen. The doctor was swathed in blankets and his head was lost in darkness.

Eluf was sitting in the antique armchair, its red leather cracked and tarnished with wear. The low-ceilinged living room was lit by table lamps and the fire that flickered in the grate. Only this morning Gideon had received the telephone call telling him that Bunny had been sighted at Heathrow Airport and five hours ago he'd announced that someone was in Bayleir Forest. Somehow she'd escaped the wraiths and the hours that had followed had been tense with waiting. But now the crash.

"You think it's her?" Eluf asked in his gruff voice.

"Undoubtedly." Gideon's voice was muffled. "I will prepare in here. Go out and investigate." He sighed, almost as if he were drinking brandy. "I will be with you in spirit."

Eluf rose from his chair and slipped out into the woods.

From his vantage point behind the fallen tree Blaine watched the doorway. Pushing over the thick, rotten trunk had required a mammoth amount of strength and he hoped it would be worth it. The slow crash as the old alder fell to the forest floor had vibrated through the trees and there was no way it couldn't have been heard in the chocolate-box cottage. He was hoping that he'd been right, that at least one of them would come out.

Blaine watched the doorway eagerly and was gratified when it opened and a tall man appeared to be putting on a jacket in the buttery light. It had begun raining harder again and thunder was growling overhead. When the bulky man stepped out onto the grass outside the cottage and shut the door behind him Blaine silently congratulated himself. Eluf might be a bodyguard but Blaine would be willing to bet he'd seen more action than the larger man ever had – if it was just the two of them Blaine could easily pick him off. Eluf started to stride towards the trees and a flash of lightning cracked down as he was halfway across the clearing. The yellow flare seemed to be directly above the cottage; the air sizzled and Blaine tasted tin. Both men looked up at the jagged piece of light punctuating the black sky and as he brought his head back down Blaine also thought he saw movement by the far corner of the house. He hoped that Bunny would find a way in quickly. The rain began falling more heavily and Blaine used the increased noise to cover the sounds he made clambering higher up the slanted trunk he was crouched on. He was thirty yards or so away from the cottage, concealed behind a thick group of trees. To see Eluf approach he had to peer out through various leaves and branches. Eluf slowly reached the edges of the trees and as he drew closer Blaine saw he was holding a gun close to his chest. The rain increased again in intensity, the droplets falling hard and fast onto Blaine's head. A dark mist began to rise behind him in the trees but Blaine was angled the wrong way to see it. He didn't turn around either - he was fully focused on the man stalking through the undergrowth before him. Eluf turned to the left, began walking away from Blaine and out of his line of sight.

Blaine swore to himself and took a stone out of his pocket. He'd picked it up just a moment before. He took aim and then threw it into a holly bush. The rustling leaves could be heard over the storm and Eluf turned back towards Blaine. The bodyguard approached the bush slowly and as he came closer Blaine levelled his gun through the trees. He crouched, narrowing his eyes for the best shot, and tried to wait until Eluf was only a few yards away from him. Eluf clearly hadn't seen him – the man was still inspecting the holly bush. The sounds of the wind rushing through the trees and the rain hitting the leaves ceased to exist for Blaine, his whole being focused on the sight down the barrel and the mark below. Tunnel vision. Blaine waited until he had a clear shot at the man's head, then gently squeezed the trigger.

Bang. The shot rang out just as thunder rolled but Blaine didn't even see what he'd hit. A hard shove pushed him forwards out of the tree and a black fog enveloped him. The wraiths were back. Blaine saw their confused outlines surround him as he battled to stand on the crackling undergrowth and waved his arms through dark green shadows. There came a roar from somewhere to his left and Eluf heavily jumped on him. The two men wrestled in the black murk and Blaine caught several fleeting impressions: a bloodied cheek, black spindly arms and brown mushy leaves. The world spun around him, a heated mess of flailing limbs and confused shadows. Suddenly in the revolving mass of impressions Blaine caught sight of his revolver half hidden beneath a mossy branch. He looked up dizzyingly and saw a wraith-arm float towards him, trailing tendrils behind it that blackened the tree he'd been sitting on. Eluf took advantage of Blaine's distraction to punch him in the kidneys but his perceptions were just as confused and the two of them were rolling seemingly uphill together when Blaine's fingers closed on the warm metal of his gun and the first wraith struck him.

Blaine screamed aloud, an animal shriek of pain, as the wraith drew its fingers across his back. The skin on his spine felt as if it had been frozen off, the pain hot and cold like a knife wound. Eluf lost his grip at the sound but Blaine hung on, the fingers of his left hand enveloped in the bodyguard's hair while the fingers of his right closed involuntarily around his gun. Another of the things touched his foot and the same unbelievable pain shot through the skin there. Blaine screamed again and convulsed as the things began attacking his calf, his side and his head. Through all of it he hung onto Eluf's scalp, even when large chunks of brown hair began falling away. Eluf was batting at him and the whole world became a mess of black rotting flesh and bloody burns until… there was a burst of pure green light - the sort that might shine through leaves into a window - and the terrible wasting ceased.

Blaine and Eluf were caught, raised up, in a nimbus of light that shone through the trees and their strange tangle of limbs was turned and twisted in the air as if being examined from every angle. In the strange, ensuing silence Blaine looked up at Eluf and saw the bodyguard's mouth open in a shocked, horrified cry that produced no sound. There was blood everywhere but no pain. The two men hung there for a terrified minute. Eluf eventually shut his mouth and looked down at Blaine with wide, petrified eyes. The two of them were sharing something that neither could comprehend. Somewhere in the background shooting streaks of blue were falling and Blaine understood that it was rain.

Just as suddenly as the experience started it was over. The nimbus was extinguished with a *clap* and the two men were dumped unceremoniously on the grass outside the front door of the cottage. They landed in a confused tangle but Blaine had enough of a survival instinct keep the gun in his hand and point it at the contents of the other. Eluf's head. He knew that he should kill him – one less man on the other side simply couldn't be a bad thing – but something in the bodyguard's expression stayed his finger on the trigger. The two of them had just shared something unbelievable and Blaine couldn't quite bring himself to kill his fellow witness in cold blood.

"It's you," Eluf said, looking up at Blaine with a pitiful expression.

"Yeah," said Blaine hoarsely. "Open the door."

Blaine stood up and held Eluf in a half-crouch by his hair beside him. Eluf reached forward and pulled the cottage door open. The two men stepped inside. Right opposite the door was a small hallway with an oval mirror hanging on the wall and Blaine caught sight of his reflection: he was covered in mud and cuts, his clothes were dirty and torn. But oh, his back… the cotton shirt had been burned through and was stuck to the blackened charred mess that had once been the skin of his right shoulder-blade. Without looking Blaine knew that his scalp and foot would be in no better condition. Eluf was in little better shape – the whole of his right ear had been blown off by Blaine's bullet even though he hadn't been attacked by the wraiths.

"Which way?" Blaine asked, knowing now that killing Faber was the only option. He could only hope that Bunny had rescued the boy in time.

"In here," croaked a voice from the living room.

Blaine's jaw hardened and he dragged Eluf with him in a vicelike grip.

"Ah," Blaine said when he entered the lounge.

In the grate the fire was still burning merrily and Gideon lay on a sofa beside it, the top of his body covered in blankets and his head hidden in shadow. Kneeling in front of him on the rag rug was Bunny. Gideon had his right arm wrapped around her neck and he held a knife tightly in the same hand.

"I wasn't expecting her to have a friend, but it makes no difference." Gideon's voice had an odd, metallic quality. "She made enough noise clambering in through the study window that my pets easily could hear her."

Bunny opened her eyes, the green irises filled with sorrow. "He had more wraiths," she whispered.

Blaine nodded, keeping his eyes on Gideon and getting a better grip on his gun. His palms were slick with sweat. "All right then. A hostage for a hostage."

Gideon laughed. "But I have nothing to lose. You think I care what happens to my servants?"

Blaine felt Eluf shift under him and took a risk. "I think you do care. He's the only one you trusted enough to bring here, right? I think you'd care very much if he were killed."

Gideon laughed again and too late Blaine saw the muzzle of the gun he held in his left hand, concealed underneath the blankets.

"No!" Blaine cried out and jumped to one side as the bullet was fired, dragging poor Eluf with him. The bullet caught the bodyguard square in the chest even as Blaine rolled forward, letting go of Eluf's scalp and moving towards Gideon. He kicked the gun out of the doctor's hand – the man seemed stunned by Eluf's death – and pointed his own revolver at Faber's head.

"Now," Blaine growled. "Drop the knife."

Strangely neither Gideon nor his hostage reacted; they were both transfixed by the sight of Eluf coughing to his death on the other side of the room. Blaine didn't even turn his head – he'd seen deaths through chest wounds before and they were never pretty. The bodyguard was coughing up blood and slowly drowning in it. Blaine realised it was quite likely that neither Bunny nor Faber had ever seen a man die before. After thirty seconds or so Eluf's wracking breaths ended and the only sound in the room was the crackling of the fire.

"Drop the knife," Blaine repeated.

Gideon smiled. Blaine could just see his mouth underneath all the blankets. "No."

"I can shoot faster than you can stab."

"Fine," replied Gideon.

Bunny shrieked when Blaine cocked his gun closer to the doctor in reply. "No!"

"What is it?" Blaine asked angrily.

"You can't kill him. He's the only one who knows how to release the boy!"

"Release him from what?"

"Look." Bunny turned slowly around in Gideon's mad embrace and pulled the blankets off him. Blaine could see that the doctor was smiling, happy for his plans to be unveiled like this. As Bunny pulled the wool off it was revealed that Gideon was not lying on the sofa at all but was instead wired up to some sort of machine that held him half-upright. He wore heart monitors with little wires stuck onto his chest through an unbuttoned shirt and a slim metal sheet curved around the lower half of his skull. The piece of metal was connected via more wires to a low machine that rested on the sofa next to him. Blaine had never seen anything like the machine before – it was covered in little blue dials and strange green gauges. It hummed lightly and the silver surface was polished to a high shine.

"What is that?" Blaine asked, leaning over to take a better look. The *Smashing Pumpkins* lyrics came back to him.

The doctor seemed to have aged ten years since Blaine had last seen him a week ago. He was now completely bald and his cheeks were wrinkled and sunken. His pallor was grey but a feverish light gleamed in his pale blue eyes.

Gideon smiled, his white lips pulled thin. "She never told you? Then why are you here?" He coughed. "I was the one paying you." Blaine's eyes flicked towards Bunny. "Ah, I see, it's all about the girl. I thought perhaps you wanted revenge on me for destroying that skyscraper while you were still in it."

Blaine wasn't about to explain the confused bundle of motives that had driven him to help Bunny, so he asked a simple question. "Why do you want to kill her?"

"Because she was the only one left who knew what we'd done. I couldn't allow this," Gideon stroked the machine lovingly, "to get into the wrong hands. So. Why are you here? Why are you helping her?"

"You've done something evil. You roped Bunny's father into it. I saw the spoon."

"What?" Gideon looked genuinely confused at the last phrase but with a shake of his head he ignored it. "I didn't rope Bunny's father into anything. It was all his idea, all of it. I merely took his theories and clothed them."

"That?" Blaine indicated the machine with the barrel of his gun, totally lost.

"N-" Gideon started, but Bunny twisted up to look at him. The knife rested on her throat, just below her chin.

"Shut up!" she cried. "I know my father, and I know his work. You may have given his theories form but you twisted them, gave them over to evil when they could have been bright. Now tell me how to save the boy!"

Gideon sat up on his pallet, holding the knife closer to Bunny's neck. He leaned forward to face her, pulling the electrodes off his chest with left hand. Spittle collected at the corners of his mouth and his eyes narrowed.

"Child, the wonderful thing in this is that all your efforts are in vain. Your beloved boy is with us no longer, he is effectively gone. Dead, deceased, passed over. A dead parrot, if you will."

"But the mist in the forest, the light just now -"

"All side effects of this little thing, I'm afraid." Gideon patted his machine. "I don't think I've quite ironed all the kinks out."

Bunny faced him with tears in her eyes but her jaw was firm. Blaine thought that maybe she knew something she wasn't telling.

Bunny stared up at the man who'd killed her father. She felt the cold blade pressed against her chin, the sweat running down her spine and her cramping leg muscles. Blaine had a moment to think: *She's never killed anyone before.* And then, with an animal snarl, Bunny brought up the gun she'd hidden inside the belt of her baggy trousers and fired straight into Gideon's torso. The doctor shouted and raised the knife up but his surprise was too great and rather than slitting Bunny's throat he succeeded only in slicing the blade up at an angle past her jaw. Blood spurted from the slash but Blaine was fairly sure it hadn't hit an artery.

"You bastard!" Bunny was screaming at the top of her voice as he collapsed back onto the sofa holding his chest. "You killed my father!"

Blaine was sure she'd claw Faber's eyes out given half a chance so he wrenched her back.

"Bunny! It's over! He's dying." It was like holding a mad woman. "Stop it!"

Eventually her struggles ceased and she sagged in his arms, watching Gideon's breaths becoming slower. He already seemed to be slipping into unconsciousness.

"You're right," she said, tears running down her cheeks. Her face was red and her t-shirt was splattered with blood. "We have to find the boy." She grabbed Blaine's hand and pulled him towards the stairs. She didn't look back at Faber. "I think he'll be up here." As they started to climb she added something odd, in a light falling voice. "I hope I recognise him. I've never met him before."

Blaine climbed the stairs slowly after her, trying to fight his increasing sense of dread. Whatever he was about to find up here would explain the madness he'd experienced over the last week. He wanted to do the right thing.

Bunny paused at the foot of the stairs and looked left and right. Directly ahead of them on the narrow landing was the open door to a bathroom but the doors on either side were shut. Bunny wiped the blood off her throat with the bottom of her t-shirt.

"We'll try right first," she said slowly, taking in the unchanged bare floorboards and yellow walls. "My father's room."

Blaine followed her as she pushed open the door. The rain could be heard louder up here, pitter-pattering on the roof. The door swung open but the large double bed inside lay empty. A men's wash bag lay discarded on the dresser and a charcoal suit jacket was draped over a chair.

"Faber's been sleeping here," Bunny said with undisguised disgust.

She clenched her fists and stalked past Blaine back out of the room. But when she reached the door on the other side of the landing she hesitated.

"Your room?" Blaine asked.

Bunny nodded, her eyes filled with tears. "And the boy's."

She pushed the door open softly and Blaine caught sight of a large, airy room with sloping ceilings and a huddle on the bed.

"Chiko?" Bunny spoke more kindly than Blaine had ever heard her. "Chiko, honey, I'm here."

There was silence for a few moments – Blaine was trying to figure out who Chiko could possibly be - and then something burst out of the wardrobe, wailing and flailing their arms.

"Hey!" Blaine reached out easily even in the dim light and caught the person as they made for the door. His shoulder killed at the movement but he ignored it. "Who are you?"

"Help! *Ayudar!*"

"Calm down!" Bunny grabbed the person and forced them to face her. The 'wraith' turned out to be a fat, wrinkled old woman who stank of fear and sweat. When the woman saw Bunny she quietened.

"You speak English?" Bunny demanded. "Who are you?"

"I know you! I see photo downstairs. My name is Rosa, Dr Faber hire me to look after boy." The woman indicated the bundle on the bed. "But I hear horrible - *temeroso* - things, I hear shooting…" Rosa's eyes were wide like a fawn trapped in headlights.

"Go to the other bedroom and wait there," Bunny ordered. "I wouldn't suggest going downstairs unless you like the look of dead bodies."

Rosa's English might not have been perfect but she understood that much well enough. She fled across the hall into the other bedroom and locked the door. "We'll worry about her later," Bunny said grimly. "Now." She moved to the edge of the bed, her face softening.

"Chiko?" she called. In the semi-darkness she could just make out the rough outline of someone under the sheets but as she got closer the light from the hallway illuminated more of the bed and she saw his face clearly for the first time. "Oh, Chiko," she breathed.

Blaine came forward to see what she was staring at. The boy lying in state was clearly Asian, with soft creamy skin and a floppy mass of black hair. He was perhaps four or five years old, he had high cheekbones and slim fingers that were spread out on the eiderdown. He was pale under his tan but still beautiful. His eyes were shut and his body was completely still. Bunny moved to touch his fingers, then quickly drew her hand away. Blaine stood on the opposite side of the bed to her and watched her study the boy. He understood little except the intensity.

"What is this, Bunny?" he said softly. "What's been going on here?"

Bunny's head was down on her chest, her blond hair fell over her face and she seemed suddenly terribly thin and worn in the shadowy bedroom. When she eventually raised her head to stare at Blaine over the still body of the child her eyes were haunted and bruised.

"Everything," she whispered slowly. "Everything that has been going on is about this boy here." She moved to touch his face but just as quickly withdrew her hand again. "He is the reason my father died, he is the reason for the madness in Tokyo and in the forest tonight. He is the reason I've just killed a man. He is all of it."

"I don't understand."

Bunny laughed, a wild sound. "I'm not sure I do either. But it seems that the time for telling is upon us, so I'll tell you what I can." She spoke in a faraway voice, a hint of bitterness playing at the edges.

Blaine nodded, still holding his gun. "So tell."

Bunny gave him one last look with her bruised eyes then opened her mouth and began.

"A year ago, Dr Gideon Faber was a moderately successful psychiatrist who'd published one or two self-help books. Enough to earn a living, enough to occasionally travel to international conferences in foreign countries. That all changed when, in the autumn of last year, he visited Japan. One of his colleagues at the conference had heard that Faber was an expert in a certain type of neurological disorder and he thought he had a patient afflicted with it. Faber agreed to visit the patient, a child, but when he met the boy he realised that he'd found something quite different, something unique. He'd found a kid who… how can I put this? Who seemed to be able to move objects outside of his body, *as if* they were his body. Does that make sense?"

"Telekinesis?"

"Yes." Bunny bit her lip. "Anyway, unsurprisingly Faber wanted to keep on seeing the boy, wanted to figure out how he did what he did. Faber did lots of research on telekinesis: read the books that describe it as a pseudo-science, read some science-fiction, watched a lot of weird documentaries. But the theory he found that really seemed to fit what was happening came from my father. My father wrote… a lot of weird philosophy. I once met a man who described it as brilliant but barking."

"Bunny -"

"No, you have to listen to this. It's complicated but it's important. It's the key to everything. My father was a necessary physicalist. That he means he thought that *everything* was in principle explainable by science. Even weird stuff like telekinesis. So he put his mind to figuring out how – *if* an episode of telekinesis could be proved without doubt to be real – such a thing might be philosophically explained."

"Okay."

"My father thought that consciousness doesn't come from an imaginary soul, it arises out of suitably complex physical objects. He thought that the mind was identical to the brain. The technical term for his sort of theory is 'supervenience' – he held that the mind was identical to the brain but not reducible to it. Sort of like… you know when you see a painting that's all made up of dots? Well, the picture supervenes on the dots – it's identical to the dots but not reducible to them. My father thought that the mind supervenes on the brain like that."

"How does that apply to telekinesis?"

"Because normally the mind arises out of a suitably complex object

– like a brain. Except my father thought that in cases of telekinesis the process was somehow happening in reverse – the mind was expanding to include physical objects that it didn't originally arise from. In other words, Chiko had somehow expanded his mind to include the objects he made to move.

"Faber loved this explanation – he thought that it fitted the facts. Now, any other doctor might want to study the boy out of curiosity or for… I don't know. For professional fame. But Faber just wanted power. He'd discovered that the boy was able to move things inside computers as well as in the real world – the possibilities for making money in today's electronic society were endless. He built a machine to increase and expand Chiko's powers, eventually he managed to improve so that he could use it himself. He tried to kidnap the boy using the machine, tried to *move* the child from where he was to where he wanted him to be. Except… it didn't work. All Faber got for his efforts was an earthquake that wrecked a city block of Tokyo and the child ran free."

"The Valentine's Day Earthquake…"

"Yeah."

"But he killed thousands of people!"

Bunny shrugged. "Yeah. And in the process he damaged the fabric of the world – the *thin* place inside the subway tunnel was at the epicentre of the earthquake. I've no doubt that after the second earthquake another one has appeared. Anyway, after that first disastrous attempt to kidnap Chiko, Faber approached my father. Luckily for him this world-expert on consciousness lived right here in good old sunny England. So Faber set up a meeting with my father and lied to him. Cooked up a whole load of hypothetical crap about what would happen *if* he found a patient with the following abilities, et cetera. My father helped him willingly and Faber learnt how to improve his machine. At some point in April Faber went to Japan and managed to retrieve the boy the old-fashioned way, by hiring people to kidnap him. Faber brought Chiko back to England and hooked him up to his new and enhanced machine. Before long Faber had his own little genie in a bottle."

Blaine was horrified. "What did Faber do to him?"

"Nothing, at first. Small things. Faber got him to move some figures around on the stock market, made him filthy rich. He kept trying to develop the machine so that he could increase the boy's abilities. You see, at this point Chiko could only move small things. Glasses, candles, books. But Faber kept boosting and boosting the machine – that's how he was able to produce those wraiths and the second, more controlled earthquake in Tokyo – and eventually one day he went too far when he hooked the boy up. Fried his brain right out of his body. Sent him comatose. Faber panicked and that's when he told my father what had really been happening. Showed him that this 'hypothetical' patient wasn't hypothetical at all but a real flesh and blood boy who'd now been hideously damaged."

"Oh my god."

"My father tried to help Chiko, he brought him here and everything, but eventually decided that the task was beyond him. So he went to Faber and told him that it had to stop, that Chiko had to be handed over to medical specialists, that it had all gone too far."

"And Faber killed him."

"Yeah." There was silence in the darkened room for a few moments.

"And Chiko?" Blaine asked the question even though he thought he knew all the answers now, knew why Bunny felt such pity for the poor brain-dead child.

But instead of giving the expected answer, Bunny bit her lip. "That's the *really* complicated bit."

Bunny reached down to stroke a lock of hair away from Chiko's forehead. When her fingertips touched his skin the world imploded.

She felt herself being tugged, pulled towards green underwater lights. Before she surrendered to it totally she heard Blaine cry out somewhere far away: "What's happening?"

"He's showing us what it was like –" Bunny tried to say, but her words were muffled and whisked away. She shut her mouth and then they were under. Bunny hung suspended in something warm and dark, feeling very conscious of her hair stirring against her neck and the feeling in her toes. And then... she was stretched. There was simply no other word for it. She felt her being rise and expand and encompass... more. At first it felt scary but then she felt lighter and freer, like she was able to breathe underwater. She moved around in this new liquid firmament, moved towards the only home she'd ever known.

The city lay before her, all bright lights shining beneath the sea. It looked powerful and magical. She swam towards it, entered it, felt that thrill of familiarity with its streetlamps and roads and buildings. The concrete stretched around her, when she flexed her shoulders buildings shook and when she breathed in breezes wound around alleyways. She felt happy, and safe, and –

A disturbance rattled through her, shook her to the core. The feeling of being larger disintegrated and a great dark shook her like a toy to deposit her somewhere else...

•

"Ahh!" Blaine screamed as a world of black surrounded him, mushrooming off the floorboards and entering his mouth and nose and eyes. It was just like the whirlwind that had happened outside of the cottage – there was no sound just thick, soft darkness. He forced himself to calm down and after a few moments was rewarded by a gentle bump on the seat of his jeans. He heard Bunny crying out to him somewhere in the distance but experienced nothing of what she did. He opened his eyes warily and his jaw fell open. He was in Tokyo.

It was night-time and Blaine sat in a dusty alley filled with broken crates and noodle cartons. Tall skyscrapers with cracking bricks rose up on either side of him, a streetlight flickered in the distance. The moon was full and rose high overhead. It was raining very softly. Somewhere far away Blaine could hear traffic and heavy metal music. He could smell rubbish and petrol.

"Blaine?" A voice called out behind him and he turned to see Bunny sitting on an up-turned garbage can.

"What the hell is going on?" he demanded.

Bunny unfolded herself and stood up slowly, looking around and breathing in the hot air with wide eyes. She was wearing the same bloodied t-shirt as before and her jeans had slipped down on her hips to show a sliver of black underwear. The gun was tucked into her belt and it was the weight of it that was pulling her trousers down. Blaine felt a sudden rush of protective desire for her, this scrawny edgy girl. Her jaw had stopped bleeding and her mouth was open in a happy smile – she looked as though she had just undergone something joyous.

"Blaine... What happened to Chiko... He just showed me. It wasn't what they thought. My father should have known, he was an expert in this stuff. He held that any organism could support consciousness if it became complex enough. Even Lego. He thought we had minds just because our brains had become complex enough to support them." Bunny suddenly jerked her head to one side. There was a rumbling in the distance and the lone streetlamp flickered out. "Blaine, look at this." She pointed into the now totally dark depths of the alley. "Do you see that?"

"What?"

"The colour. The colour of the shadows."

Blaine blinked. "Oh god." He didn't see it, and then he did.

All of the black shadows shaded to green in their centres, as if all of the darkness was lit from within. Once he saw it he couldn't un-see it. The colour was everywhere. Everything from the discarded chopsticks in the gutter to Bunny's boots to the edges of the buildings was surrounded in

•

a faint green nimbus of light. Even the slowly falling raindrops glittered green as they fell.

"Blaine," Bunny whispered. "When Faber, with my father's help, racked up that machine they didn't blow Chiko's brain. They just... blew it out. Like a huge expanding jellyfish of consciousness, floating in the void. And where did it float to? Tokyo. The only place the poor child had ever known.

"My father wrote that even Lego could become conscious if its parts were assembled to a suitable degree of complexity. Well, what's more complex than a city?"

There was silence and a newspaper floated past them on a sudden breeze. "Jesus."

"The Tokyo street children have a legend – a kind of superstition – about the city. They say it is alive, that it has a soul. A sort of monster. They call it the *Tokai-Kaibutsu*. That's what Chiko became. He made it real. He is identical to the city, his mind supervenes on it like it used to do on his brain."

"Jesus," Blaine said again. He touched the brick wall beside him to steady himself. "How do you *know* all this? How do you know all this when Faber didn't?"

"Chiko told me," said Bunny in an even quieter voice. "The day I found my father dead he made contact with me. He made a statue fly in the shrine, helped me to escape from Faber's wraiths. It was just images, just impressions. But he told me he felt sorry for my father, he hadn't understood what was happening then but he did now and he didn't want Faber to kill me too. It helped that I'm a schoolteacher. It made it easier for him to trust me. He convinced me to run to Tokyo, he thought he could protect me there." Bunny ran her hand lovingly down the wall of the nearest building. "And, for a long time, he did."

"But when I found you –"

"I couldn't cope, okay!" Her eyes flashed. "My father had just died and I'd entered some sort of, of fairytale and I didn't cope very well. At least, not completely. Getting high helped. Don't you dare judge me."

"I'm not, I swear." Blaine held out his hands in a pacifying gesture. "But, Bunny, why are we here? Where *are* we?" Thunder rolled somewhere in the distance.

Bunny chewed on her lower lip. "I know *where* we are. We're inside Chiko's mind. And no, I don't know if we're actually in Tokyo but it's as near as damnit as makes no difference. But why we're here..." she looked around again. It seemed to Blaine that he could feel the ground vibrating through the soles of his feet. "Blaine, I think he's afraid."

"What? Why?"

And then they found out.

Striding over the horizon, like the iron man of yore, came a thirty foot high wraith-version of Dr Faber. His features weren't clear but the glasses and the hawk nose stood out clearly through the black gaseous mass that made up his figure. Everywhere he walked buildings crumbled to dust.

"No!" Bunny shrieked. "You're killing Chiko!"

"How is Faber doing this?" Blaine cried. He was now fighting for balance in the juddering alleyway – the city felt like it was undergoing an earthquake.

"He must not be dead! He must have heard us talking and he's used the machine somehow, to come here!"

"I see." Blaine locked his jaw and touched the gun still jammed into his trousers. "So the bastard just didn't die quick enough."

"Chiko!" Bunny was crying. "You just have to hold on a bit more! I shot him - he can't live much longer!"

For just a second Blaine thought the earthquake ceased in answer to her plea. And then the tremors were back and Bunny was grabbing him by the hand, pulling him away from his terrified study of the goliath bearing down on them.

"C'mon!" she was screaming, yanking Blaine after her as she *jumped* through the brick wall of the alley which was suddenly as malleable as wax.

They dived through the suffocating blackness and emerged into a warehouse on the other side. They could hear the crashing sounds of destruction behind them and they sprinted through the concrete rooms as fast as they could, Blaine noticing Bunny's limp but knowing there was nothing he could do. Inside the warehouse they came to another dead end and Bunny *pulled* them through the wall into another alley. They sprinted through it, two passing wraiths themselves in the dark, when Bunny slipped on a broken bottle and she went over with a cry.

"Quick!" Blaine urged, already seeing the shadow of the goliath looming over the far buildings.

"I can't," Bunny gasped. "You go."

"I won't leave you." Blaine picked her up in a fireman's lift and looked back over his shoulder.

The giant was gaining on them. The Faber-wraith smashed its mammoth legs through buildings and streets and walls that collapsed into piles of black ash at its passage. Blaine tried to run but Bunny was just too heavy and he couldn't leave her. Eventually he too fell and as he lay there hitching for breath, trying to summon the strength to rise again, he looked up into the mad face of the goliath and realised it was nearly upon them.

The Faber-wraith raised its shadowy foot high to bring it down and crush them, ash flickering in its wake, and Blaine saw it coming closer and closer until it was only a foot away from his face. He screamed, his mouth open and his cheeks white in the face of it, and then the foot imploded from within.

The whole Faber-wraith exploded, raining black fluttery bits of dust onto the street that floated, harmlessly, to the ground.

The walls of the alleyway seemed to glow green and Blaine looked down at Bunny in his arms.

With his face and hair covered in ash, Blaine spoke. "I guess," he said carefully, "that the old bastard finally died."

Bunny squealed – something between a laugh and a sob – and buried her face in his chest. Blaine held her and watched the dark shadows of the green city dance. He shut his eyes and when he opened them he *knew* they were back in the cottage in Pottersby.

"We're here," he whispered, and was deeply gratified to see Bunny smile at him. Then, with a different look on her face, she pulled herself up off the floor and onto the bed.

"Oh, Chiko," she whispered. "You're safe now. But I do so wish you'd come back."

There was no response except the gentle rise and fall of the boy's chest and Blaine was about to put a comforting hand on Bunny's shoulder when a miracle happened.

Chiko opened his eyes.

Bunny gasped and put a hand to the boy's cheek. Chiko smiled - the expression calm and happy - and with his right hand he pointed weakly to the skylights above his head. Dawn was just breaking and sunlight was filtering through the green leaves on the trees outside. Bunny turned to stare and she smiled too when she saw what was materialising on the windowpane.

On the frosty glass a great ice dragon was curling its tail and grinning.

EPILOGUE

The mind drifts in ether, tugged past sunken stars into ever darker swathes of sea-green. Everything here is green. The creature observes its world through a bottle-green lens, accustomed now to the way the shadows shade to indigo and the star-coronas are edged with silver.

Chiko's consciousness floats through the glimmering firmament on a train of green stars, gliding through the air above the city and sinking at will into the ocean's depths. The one is filled with shooting lights and the other with tiny darting fish. Chiko is happy that he has been freed from the madman's machinations, happy that his best friend has finally attained revenge for her father. Sometimes he thinks of the cottage in the forest where his best friend and her Irishman are making their home; Gideon Faber was charged with Robert Eury's murder and even though the police could make little sense of the other two deaths that occurred in the house they have been ruled as a murder-suicide. Chiko's best friend doesn't know it but he 'moved' some paperwork to make everything go smoother for them. He even tried to heal them, but although neither are crippled they will bear their scars for life. Bunny will forever limp on her twisted knee and Blaine has silvery burns on his scalp, shoulder-blade and foot. Chiko doesn't think they mind. Bunny is working on a posthumous publication of her father's last work and Blaine is looking to re-join the police force. Although Chiko is happy that his friends are happy he is mostly happy for himself: he has been reunited with his parents in Tokyo. He has been spoiled with gifts and kisses, he has missed his family dearly.

Chiko still needs his city, though. At night his mind detaches gently from his body - like a boat floating from a mooring - and he soars over the glittering metropolis.

Chiko is very happy indeed, drifting on forever and ever underneath the stars through the underwater lights of his green city.

AUTHOR BIOGRAPHY

Emily Thomas is a young author who has lived most of her life in the Channel Islands. She is currently studying at Christ's College, Cambridge for a PhD in Philosophy. She enjoys writing metaphysics papers almost as much as she enjoys writing fiction. Her academic career has been punctuated by periods of extensive travel and she has backpacked on a shoestring budget around every continent in the world. The Green City is Emily's first published novel and she is already working on a second.